WITCH HUNT

A Preternatural Affairs Novel

SM REINE

OTHER SERIES BY SM REINE

The Descent Series

The Ascension Series

Seasons of the Moon

The Cain Chronicles

The characters and events portrayed in this book are fictitious. Any similarity to real persons, living or dead, is coincidental and not intended by the author.

This book is sold DRM-free so that it can be enjoyed in any way the reader sees fit. Please keep all links and attributions intact when sharing. All rights reserved.

http://authorsmreine.com/

Copyright © SM Reine 2014
Published by Red Iris Books
1180 Selmi Drive, Suite 102
Reno, NV 89512

Witch Hunt

SM Reine

CHAPTER ONE

HELL OF A NIGHT.

It was my first thought when I peeled my eyelids open—an immediate precursor to "everything hurts" and "screw tequila, I'm never drinking alcohol again." My mouth was dry like I'd licked that brown apartment carpeting that every sadistic landlord inflicts on his tenants, including me. My muscles were petrified into knots.

Somehow, I stretched my legs out, flexed my toes, twisted my hips. My spine popped a few times. My body creaked.

And something jangled.

Would you look at that? A pair of open handcuffs dangled from my headboard. The key glistened on the bedside table, reflecting a sunbeam right into my aching eyeballs. I didn't make a habit of decorating my bedroom with my work equipment, so I assumed that recreational use of my cuffs meant I had company. The best kind of company.

I swatted it with a finger and grinned at the clatter of chains.

My eyes traveled from the cuffs to my arm.

Four bloody scratches spanned the space between wrist and elbow.

I'd handled enough crime scenes to recognize fingernail marks. And I'd been with enough women to know that some wildcats liked it like that.

Yeah, definitely a hell of a night.

Too bad I couldn't remember it.

Grabbing at the scraps of memory made them float away faster. I thought I remembered a beautiful woman with beautiful curves and the kind of throaty giggle that would make me instantly hard. I had half a stalk just trying to remember her.

I sat up, checked the clock. I was late for work. Twenty minutes late, in fact. Should have woken up hours ago, showered, put on my monkey suit, gone into the office. No way I would be in before lunch now. Talk about an instant boner-killer.

Standing hurt in all the bad ways. My throbbing skull made my nuts shrivel into my body. Worst hangover I've ever had? Probably. There wasn't much competition. I wasn't a drinking guy. If I'd been partying this hard last night, she must have been really worth it.

Where was she, anyway?

I was alone in my bedroom. The open windows cast unforgiving beams of yellow light on the wall, cut into slices by my mini-blinds. The curtains were open. The neighborhood must have gotten a pretty good show.

But there was no woman in sight—no souvenirs but a misused pair of cuffs and a backache.

Out of habit, I opened my side drawer and grabbed a poultice that I'd prepared on the last full moon. Only two of them left. I'd need to do another ritual soon. I popped one into my mouth, chewed the grave dirt and oak, felt my muscles warm with magic. I grimaced as I swallowed. It was about as pleasant as drinking the clumps at the bottom of a protein shake.

I scratched a few unflattering itches as I snagged a suit out of my closet. Looked like I needed to steam out the wrinkles while I showered. Always did. I wasn't good at getting my clothes out of the dryer in time, and government work didn't pay well enough to justify the dry cleaners.

I hung it over my arm and dismantled the wards on my bedroom door with a wave of my hand. Or at least, I tried to dismantle the wards, but they weren't active. I must have forgotten to turn them on during my drunken haze.

As soon as I stepped out and saw the rest of my apartment, I gave a low whistle.

My kitchen was a wreck. The contents of the counters had been dumped on the linoleum. The unplugged microwave was upside down on the toaster like they were the ones having a hot tryst. My jar of dried beans had shattered and spilled its guts all the way into the living room. The Blu-rays were everywhere. Oh man, even my eight-track collection had been screwed up.

There were stains on my couch and I didn't want to know what they were. Lubricant or bodily fluids or whatever. The damn thing was from IKEA anyway. I would just toss it and get another one.

Again, I tried to remember the night before, and failed.

"Hope you were worth it," I muttered, mentally tallying the cost of restoring my collections.

Fortunately, my fire safe was untouched, and my badge for work and my wallet were still on the bookshelf. I took a quick inventory of the contents. Cash, driver's license, genuine counterfeit FBI identification, unmarked key card, St. Benedict's medallion. Everything in its proper place.

My apartment had been turned upside down by a mysterious woman, but at least she had been honest about it.

Something out of place caught my eye. Not something that had gone missing, but something that didn't belong to me.

A Glock.

I was already right in front of the bathroom when I saw the gun on my coffee table, so the unpleasant shock of possessing a firearm I didn't recognize was interrupted by another kind of shock.

The floor in front of the bathroom door squished. I stepped back and lifted a foot to see what I'd touched.

It was red. It was slick. It smelled like a slab of rare steak.

It definitely wasn't lubricant.

Once I realized that I smelled meat, I smelled more of it. It was thick in my sinuses. I wasn't just nauseous because of the stiff neck and the hangover; I was nauseous because I smelled something dead.

In my apartment.

Funny how much faster I could move once I'd stepped in a puddle of blood.

I slipped back into the living room, dropped my suit on the chair, grabbed the Louisville Slugger from where it was propped on the wall. Everything was so much brighter and clearer than it had been a few seconds ago. My heart was hammering and every beat was a shot of adrenaline.

As I curled my fists around the bat, my peripheral vision seemed like it widened. The whole world was quiet. The air conditioning clicked on and cool air whispered against my ankles.

The apartment narrowed to the bathroom door as I approached. I didn't hear anything moving on the other side.

I opened it.

The blood into the carpet was the end of a smear that crossed the linoleum and terminated at the other end of my bathroom—which, until that second, had been my favorite room in the apartment. The toilet and counter and fluorescent lights were standard Home Depot cheapies, but the bathtub was not. It was one of those big corner tubs with the jets that feel like sin after a hard workout at the gym. I'm enough of a man to admit to loving a hot bath. Sometimes even with bubbles and fizzy salts.

And there was the woman that had given me such a wild ride. Legs like a colt. Firm, perky breasts. The kind of pouty lips my eldest brother, Domingo, used to call "beejay mouth" until I punched him hard enough to shut his stupid face.

The mystery woman was real pretty. I knew her name—I was sure I knew her name. For sure she worked at The Olive Pit, a favorite bar for my office. It was where we relaxed on Fridays at six o'clock and held retirement parties and the annual Christmas gift exchange.

This waitress had laughed at me the first time I asked for her name, and the second time, and the third, but eventually I wised up and just took a look at the schedule in the kitchen. I couldn't remember making love to those long legs and perfect breasts, but I remembered her ridiculously feminine handwriting.

Erin. Her name was Erin, punctuated with a smiley face encircled by a heart.

She was dead in my bathtub.

Hell of a night.

CHAPTER TWO

MY NAME'S CÈSAR HAWKE. I'm a witch working for a division of the government you've never heard about.

The world's not what everyone thinks it is—unless you think that our world's a pawn in a game of chess between Heaven and Hell, and riddled with as much magic and wonder as it is with evil.

In that case, the world is exactly what you think.

My place of employment—the Office of Preternatural Affairs—takes a modern approach to an ages-old problem. It used to be that inquisitors would burn demons and the people in league with them. Now we get warrants, perform arrests, put the suspects on trial, and send guilty parties back to the Hell from whence they came with the travel forms filled out in triplicate.

Everything you've ever heard about demons, angels, and witches is true. I would know. I'm a witch myself. But the world's in denial about us. The Industrial Revolution brought about an era of people too smart to believe in the boogeyman and everyone has spent long decades telling themselves comforting lies about the mundane world they think they live in. Aside from some priests, renegade demon hunters, and victims of demonic crime, nobody knows the truth.

Nobody but me and the other magically inclined special agents I work with, anyway. And we work hard to keep it that way.

This stuff I do with the OPA, it saves lives on most days.

Most days, I said.

I was still standing in the bathroom doorway and didn't know how long I'd been like that. My arms were hurting from holding the bat with such a tight grip. My breaths were choppy and loud. It was the white roar of an approaching tornado.

Erin had long, lacquered fingernails that were attached to long, shapely arms that were draped over the side of my previously favorite bathtub. The nail on her right-hand ring finger was missing. The one on her pinkie was cracked. They were the kind of fingernails that would leave gouges on a man's arm during sex if she was having a real good time—or if she was trying to fight off a murderer.

Glancing at the scratches on my arm a second time didn't fill me with the same proud warmth it had the first time.

Swallowing down the acid taste of bile, I took another step into the bathroom, careful not to smear the blood more than I already had. I needed a better look at what had happened in my apartment—in my damn *home*.

Her head was tipped back against the tile, so it was easy to see the startlingly dark bruises wrapped around her throat. They formed a perfect imprint of two long-fingered hands that must have seized her from behind.

At a glance, it was hard to say if it was the strangulation that killed her or if it was the gunshot wound positioned directly between the globes of her breasts. I did feel safe guessing that the gunshot wound was where all the blood came from, though.

The Glock on my table.

I was suddenly in motion again, lifting the baseball bat, moving through an apartment that suddenly felt like six hundred square feet of deathtrap.

My search for an intruder was short and fruitless. The closets seemed deep and dark and endless even though they were too small to hold all my TV show Blu-rays, much less a murderer. I opened every kitchen cabinet and there was obviously nobody in there, either. I just about tripped over my free weights as I searched behind the bloody couch—yeah, that was blood on the cushions, all right.

Aside from poor Erin and a Glock that wasn't mine, I was alone in my apartment.

My cell phone appeared in my hand. I dialed without looking at it as I walked back to the bathroom. I didn't want to see her like that again, but it seemed too cruel to leave her alone.

Staring at Erin, all I could think about was Ofelia. Erin didn't look anything like my sister, who was dark-haired, like me, and only an inch shy of six feet. All Hawkes were tall like that. Erin was a short redhead, ivory-skinned and lean. But I looked at Erin, and all I could see was Ofelia with her bloody neck and bruised, lumpy face, and I was filled with a burning hate at myself, hate at the world, hate for the tequila that had wiped my memory of what had happened here.

The phone stopped ringing. Switched to a voice.

"You're late, Cèsar, and I'm going to have your nuts on a griddle for it. Little salt, lots of pepper, maybe some—"

"There's a dead body in my bathtub, Suzy," I interrupted.

Silence.

I probably should have called OPA dispatch or something, but I didn't want to talk to dispatch; I wanted to talk to my officemate. She would get it. She would know what to do, how I should react, the steps we needed to take to fix it. Her head was always clearer than mine.

"You're going to have to say that again." She sounded so calm, but there was a hard edge to her voice. Suzume Takeuchi—Suzy to me—was usually unflappable. But I think I'd just flapped her.

"You heard me. There's a body in my bathtub. You gotta head down here with a Union unit. We've gotta pull this scene apart and figure out what the hell happened."

Another long pause, and then, "Did you kill her?"

The question hit me between the eyes.

Scratches on my arm, body in my apartment, no memories in my skull—it hadn't even occurred to me that I might have forgotten about killing Erin.

The idea was so ridiculous that I almost felt like I should laugh.

Almost.

"No, I didn't kill her," I said. "Who do you think I am?"

If she answered, I didn't hear it. I was distracted by the wail of sirens through the cracked bathroom window. They were distant but approaching fast.

It wasn't the Union, which was like a special forces arm of the OPA. The Union didn't blast through residential zones with sirens wailing. They were covert ops. They rolled in with black helicopters and black SUVs and quietly arrested or assassinated the guilty.

Since it wasn't the Union, those sirens belonged to the LAPD. The mundane police force.

Someone had called the damn cops on me.

"I need a Union unit *now*, Suzy." I set down the Louisville Slugger and went to my living room window. It was a beautiful spring day. The oak tree blocking half my view was budding. Some kids that lived in the complex were playing on the grass. I could see the flash of lights beyond them.

Suzy seemed to understand why I was suddenly more urgent. "Okay, Cèsar, don't do anything crazy. I'll take this straight to Director Friederling. Cooperate with the police; we'll be there shortly." And then she hung up on me without saying goodbye because Suzy never said goodbye.

I pulled on the first clothes I found—boxer briefs, a pair of gray sweatpants with my alma mater's logo on the hip, a white t-shirt—and that was when I heard footsteps coming up the stairs outside.

Every instinct told me to prepare to fight and run. I hadn't done anything wrong. I shouldn't have felt guilty. But I was the one with the scratches on my arm and bloody feet, and I knew what they were going to think. I wasn't authorized to tell these people that I was with the Office of Preternatural Affairs. Officially speaking, the OPA and I didn't exist.

All the cops were going to see was a man who got drunk off his ass and killed a woman.

But if I ran, if I resisted—like the burn of adrenaline in my veins wanted me to do—they were going to see a man who had killed a woman and was fighting them. It'd be as good as digging myself a nice, deep grave.

I had to cooperate. That was what Suzy said. "Cooperate with the police; we'll be there shortly." Like I had any other option.

Then my door was getting kicked open, there were hands forcing me to the floor, and I was handcuffed.

And mostly, I was just thinking that I was *definitely* never drinking tequila again.

CHAPTER THREE

THE POLICE STATION KIND of smelled like piss. You know, ammonia. That chemical in urine that seemed to be impossible to scrub away once the puddle went dry. I could smell bleach, too—someone trying to clean up someone else's mess.

Seemed like that was going to be a theme for the week.

It wasn't the first time I'd been there. When Domingo got picked up for tagging in high school, that was where they had brought him: 77th Street Community Police Station. They were cool guys. They knew the neighborhood, they knew the kids, they knew who belonged and who didn't. I didn't know any of them by name anymore—it had been a long time since Domingo had gotten into that kind of trouble—but the cops walking me through the front door had the same honest faces that the old guys did.

They marched me past some desks that looked a lot like mine. The desks were covered in paperwork and staffed by exhausted men just trying to make the world a better place, when the world didn't want to be made any better. They were underfunded and overscheduled and stressed out, just like I was.

But I wasn't on the desk side of things now. The paperwork wasn't my problem now. What had happened at my apartment—that was someone else's bureaucratic nightmare.

The holding cell had a bench and a toilet and a barred window. The one next door had a couple of gang bangers that looked like they had won a fight. The right side of one guy's face was purple, and the other one was bleeding through the bandages on his ribs. Whatever had happened to them, they were in good enough shape to be in jail. That meant they'd won.

The cops were polite about putting me in the holding cell and locking the door behind me. No manhandling or anything, just took off the cuffs and sat me down.

"I need a phone call," I said.

One of my escorts said, "We'll see what we can do."

I wish I'd told them in the car that I worked for the FBI—the currently accepted cover story for OPA agents—because I was hesitant to say it after having met my two new roommates. I mean, I was an intimidating guy. I benched twice my body weight, my body fat was less than ten percent, and I looked like a freaking tank in gray sweat pants. But two gang members with stylized crosses on their throats and "SUR 13" on their foreheads weren't going to be hot on chilling in a holding cell with a Fed. The next couple hours of my life would be easier if I kept my cover story to myself.

Once the cops were gone, there was nothing to do but read these guys' life stories inked into their skin. I didn't know human gang signs well. Give me a witch wearing chains of crystals and medallions, I could tell you his coven affiliation, status in the witching community, and even his favorite spells to cast. But a sad-looking Jesus, some elaborate crosses, eighteens and thirteens—I had no clue.

They didn't think much of my staring. They stared back. Hard.

I wished I'd brought my last strength poultice with me when I'd gotten arrested.

I didn't belong in jail. I wasn't this guy. I wasn't the one with the tats bleeding from an alleyway knife fight. Even when I'd gotten caught up in trouble with Domingo, it'd been property crime. Not this violent crap.

Bloody Face started cajoling me in Spanish. Whatever he was saying, it was probably offensive. I wouldn't know. When Abuela Teresa had come from San Salvador two generations back, she made sure all her kids spoke English. My parents, aunts, and uncles had never spoken Spanish, so I definitely didn't. But I still had the looks, and these guys weren't the first to think they could talk with me in "our" native language.

It was easy to tune out words I didn't understand. It faded into the background of distant voices. I stretched out on the bench, folded my hands over my chest, focused on the window.

Sky was turning gray. Looked like rain.

My memory of finding Erin in the bathroom swelled to the surface.

Erin. *Jesus, Erin.*

I had ridden along on a couple of murder scenes when I was in training for the OPA. Everyone did their time with the Union whether they liked it or not, and it was always unforgettable. I remembered the stuff that they looked for in deaths related to demons. There were often runes and seals, finger painting with blood, that kind of stuff. Smarter demons, the ones more like humans, often liked to carve into their prey. The dumber ones just ate them.

Erin hadn't been eaten. She hadn't been carved. There were no runes in my bathroom. Just a hole in her heart and hand-shaped bruises stamped onto her throat.

It looked like any mundane murder I'd seen on those CSI TV shows. Nothing to do with demonic possession or magic or a hungry fiend whose master had lost control. It looked like someone had fucked her, choked her, shot her. All stuff that a human could easily do—anyone with a grudge.

I refused to think of that "anyone" as me. I was a victim here. It was the only possible truth, and the only one I would consider.

Something touched my feet and I looked up to see Bloody Shirt making kissy faces at me. He was pressed up against the bars. Leaning toward me, harassing me with gestures instead of words.

I propped up my knees so they couldn't reach me. Shut my eyes. I still had a hangover and none of this was making me feel any better about it.

WITCH HUNT

Guess with what happened to Erin, I should have been grateful that I was alive to feel so fucking miserable.

I told myself, *Count your blessings, Cèsar, because the day is going to get worse before it gets better.*

Sometimes it sucked to be right.

Yesterday had been so much better.

I'd just wrapped up a four-month-long manhunt for a witch named Black Jack who had a quick hand for tarot and a quicker hand for curses. Most of those curses were dumb pranks—might mess with someone's head, but nothing deadly. The numbers in the OPA's budget were redder than blood, so he'd been on the observation list for years without anyone managing to justify the cost of hunting him down.

Until he cursed some car keys and his ex-girlfriend drove into oncoming traffic.

That had bumped his priority up real fast.

The New Mexico office sent the file to us and Black Jack landed on my desk. Long story short, I bagged him just like I'd bagged a half a dozen other witches this year. Picked him up in a gas station. Slipped a mix of a sleeping and paralysis potion in his energy drink, knocked him out cold.

That was the result of four months of hunting on my part and years of monitoring by other agents. Taking Black Jack off the streets meant that we'd be saving a lot of money on cleaning up his bullshit. It meant we might actually get merit increases on our paychecks next summer.

Yeah, the big boss had been happy with me, and so was everyone else.

That was why I had been at The Olive Pit last night even though I don't drink. We were riding high on the knowledge that Black Jack was going to Italy for trial, never to be our problem again. Everyone had been there: Fritz Friederling, the director who had given me the job with the OPA; some hunters with the Union; all the other investigators in the Magical Violations Department; even the administrative assistants.

Suzy had been there, too. The amount of alcohol that woman could put away was incredible considering she was five feet tall in heels. She had been exchanging crass jokes with Joey and Eduardo, the kind of stuff that I would never say in front of a lady, and playing drinking games that started with setting shots on fire and ended up with us all getting completely trashed.

I hadn't paid for a single drink. All the guys had been buying for me—the man who nailed Black Jack.

They had given me shit over the way tequila made me cough and choke. Suzy had been pounding her tiny, delicately boned fist on my back and it had felt kind of like a jackhammer.

Bad alcohol, great company. So I had been feeling good. Real good.

Then Erin had arrived for her shift. She'd had a nasty black eye covered up with makeup. Big bruise. It covered half of her face. I remembered when my sister, Angela, was trying to cover up the evidence of her abuse, so I'd known immediately what was going on.

I had cornered Erin by the kitchen. I'd said something like, "Tell me who's messing with you, and I'll take care of it." Big words coming from a drunk guy, but I'd meant it.

"Nobody's messing with me," she had said. She'd batted her eyelashes at me. Shot me a sweet smile. "I'm okay."

"Let me help you," I'd insisted. And then I'd told her who I was, whom I worked for, how I could nail the guy that was hurting her. I shouldn't have told her the truth, but I did.

Then there was a haunted, hungry look in her eyes. Just for a second. Nothing more than a flash of it.

"I'll think about it," she'd said.

Suzy had found me, dragged me back to drinking. We'd played a few more games. I noticed at some point that Fritz had left and thought that was probably my cue to leave, too. Whenever the director thinks it's time to get home and sleep, it's time to sleep. But Suzy had talked me into staying.

Erin brought me a drink toward the end of the night. When she'd dropped it off, she kissed me on the cheek, slipped me a note. "I'll tell you after my shift. Maybe you can help. But not here. Your place."

When she'd left, I checked what she had given me.

Her phone number.

Then I'd tossed back the fireball she'd given me. I'd felt hot and excited at the thought of having Erin in my apartment. Suzy had been talking to me but I'd barely even seen her lips moving, much less understood what she was saying. My head was filled with liquored haze and the buzz of knowing I'd be taking a beautiful woman home.

After that…well, I guess Erin had come home with me, and I think we might have had sex.

I knew I hadn't helped her.

I couldn't remember that part.

You always thought if you got in trouble working for the OPA, it was going to be when you crossed someone like Black Jack. You thought it was going to be having a curse slipped under your desk or a demon assassin crawling out of the darkest alleys of Helltown.

I'd never thought it would be like this.

CHAPTER FOUR

THEY GOT THE OTHER guys out of the holding cell before they came for me. I was alone with my view of the drizzly spring day for about an hour. Just me and my thoughts and a determined sparrow shrieking. It was kind of nice. Meditative.

Then life was moving again. There were people at my door and the halls were sliding past me. More desks, lots of guards, locked doors.

They dropped in an interview room.

It was hot in there. It couldn't have been more than sixty degrees outside, but it was ninety between those four unremarkable walls, and I was immediately sweating. Hard to say if the discomfort was meant to be a technique to loosen me up or if the LAPD just didn't have a budget for fixing the A/C. Either way, I didn't like it. I still wanted my phone call.

Instead, they were gonna interrogate me.

You couldn't call them "interrogations" anymore, though, because we didn't "interrogate" people. That was too aggressive. That assumed too much guilt. We *interviewed* suspects these days.

Whatever we called it—whatever the LAPD called it—I knew exactly where I was and what was about to happen to me. And I knew it wasn't going to be fun or pretty.

Back at OPA headquarters, we had several interview rooms. One of them had a silver-reinforced door and silver chains and a silver chair, just in case we crossed paths with a werewolf and needed to "interview" them. One of them was warded against magic, nullifying any witch that might sneak a charm in with her. Another had crosses and the pendant of St. Benedict engraved into the concrete floor—that one was for the demon-possessed perps.

But this place was almost hilariously normal. One-way mirror. Table in the middle with two chairs on one side and a single chair on the other—that was for me. The door wasn't magicked or silver or anything. I got a good look at the completely normal lock as they guided me inside. They didn't even have wards to nullify the magic in the poultice I had consumed that morning.

Two detectives came in to talk with me. I wondered how many were on the other side of the window. I wondered if they were scared of how big I was, how messy Erin's body had been, how little they could find about me with a background check.

"You like to drink, Mr. Hawke?" asked the first detective. Her name was Kearney.

"I'd like a water, yeah," I said.

That wasn't what they meant, but they got me a glass of water anyway. Tasted like it had been sitting in a plastic jug for months.

"You drank a lot last night," Kearney went on. She was an intense woman with a square jaw and no waistline. Fists clenched on top of the table. "When we tested you this afternoon, your blood alcohol level was still above legal limits for driving."

I didn't want to talk about my drinking habits. I didn't *have* drinking habits.

"I need my phone call," I said again. Felt like I'd been saying nothing else since they'd brought me here.

"Where do you work?" asked the other detective, Ramirez. He was a skinny man with gray hair.

I didn't even have to think about the fake answer. It was habit now. "I work for the Federal Bureau of Investigation."

They didn't look surprised by that answer, so someone had already found my fake FBI badge.

"What do you do for the FBI, exactly?"

"It's classified." So much more classified than they could ever know. They lived in a small world, an ordinary world. They didn't know anything.

Identifying myself as an FBI agent was usually enough to get me out of any degree of trouble. It didn't work that day. Not after Erin, and not with Kearney shooting daggers out of her eyeballs at me. "I'm sure that must be stressful," she said. "Working for the FBI, doing secret work. You have to unwind somehow. Who can blame you?"

I kept my mouth shut.

"How often do you think you go to the bar called The Olive Pit? Three times a week, four times? Every day? Just on Fridays? How much does it take to help you unwind, Mr. Hawke?"

I knew this routine. I'd done it a few times myself. They were trying to establish a narrative. They would try to set me up as a woman-beating alcoholic, tell me I got piss-drunk and killed Erin, try to sneak into it sideways so that I wouldn't even realize I was agreeing until I'd signed the confession. You'd be surprised how easily people would admit guilt when they thought someone understood them.

But I wasn't going to give them anything. They knew that I could ask for a lawyer at any minute and the interview would come to an end.

Thing is, I didn't want my lawyer. I had nothing to defend.

I wanted the men in black suits to roll in here and erase me.

"Who does the Glock belong to?" I asked Kearney, addressing her directly. "Did you check the serial numbers?"

"Don't you think it's kind of strange to have a gun on your coffee table and no idea whom it belongs to?"

"Yeah, I sure do," I said.

"You have a gun safe in your apartment."

And I had a gun in it, too. A Desert Eagle. They wouldn't know that, though, because I'd warded the safe with the help of some of the OPA's best witches, and nobody could open it but me. Seeing the stuff in there would have made Kearney grow chest hair.

"I use it for my china collection." I didn't smile

when I said it.

Disbelief was etched all over their faces, but they didn't challenge me on it. Why bother pushing? They thought they had all day. Really, they only had until Suzy came in with her backup.

I hoped Suzy was close.

"A heavy-drinking FBI agent with a china collection," Kearney said.

"I like breaking stereotypes."

"Tell me about how you got the scratches on your arms." The order came rapid-fire, almost talking over me. Trying to startle me into answering.

I turned my arms over so I could look at them. They had swabbed the scratches when I'd first arrived. Took a DNA sample out of my mouth and a vial of blood, too. The scratches had hurt the most. They were still tender.

I didn't have an answer for them, and I wouldn't have given it if I did.

"How long have you been thinking about killing Erin Karwell?" asked Kearney.

I slammed my fists on the table. I knew better, but I couldn't help it. "I didn't kill Erin."

"Relax, Agent Hawke," Ramirez said. "It seems like you've got a lot of pent-up aggression."

Yeah, I was feeding right into the damn narrative.

The way he said "agent," it sounded like he was referring to a piece of shit stuck to the sole of his shoe. He didn't think much of federal agents, did he?

The pissing contest between local and federal

government was an eternal battle. I'd seen it play out in a dozen different states—any time that I had to cooperate with the cops and deal with all the bullshit that followed.

They didn't like having the feds fuck with their business, and they were taking it out on me.

It had to be that because there was no way anyone would really believe I'd kill a woman.

Problem was, I wasn't who they thought I was. And I shouldn't have even been there.

Where the hell was Suzy?

Kearney opened her mouth to ask another question, but I was tired of questions.

"I want my lawyer," I said.

Interview over.

CHAPTER FIVE

I DIDN'T CALL MY lawyer. I didn't even *have* a lawyer. Who needed one when the OPA had the best legal department that taxpayer dollars could buy?

Instead, I called Suzy. I was ticked off when she was at her desk to answer it. I'd been imagining her leading the cavalry to come and save me, riding in on her metaphoric white horse, and instead she was in our damn cubicle.

"Cèsar. It's you." Her tone didn't inspire confidence.

I took a quick glance over my shoulder to make sure Kearney wasn't on my ass. She was at the nearby desk filling out paperwork. Ramirez was watching me, eyes wary, patiently watchful, but too distant to hear a whisper.

I twisted my wrists, trying to get comfortable with the phone. My wrists were cuffed again and I was getting real sick of it. "What's going on, Suzy? Why am I still here?"

It took her a long time to answer.

"I'm sorry, Cèsar."

My heart sank all the way down to my sneakers. Her tone was enough to tell me that the OPA wasn't coming. No men in black to make me disappear. Nobody to say that I was innocent, this had all been a misunderstanding, their files were forfeit.

"Do you have guys at my apartment? Are they investigating?"

"Yeah. We've gotten involved, but the Union is handling the investigation."

Bad sign. Union procedure was a secret, even to me, but they only got called in when the shit had hit the fan more than usual. "And?"

A sigh. "It looks bad. Real bad."

"You know I didn't do this, Suzy."

"It doesn't matter what I know. It matters what everyone else thinks. Look, I can hook you up with my lawyer. He's a good guy. He's done criminal law before, and if anyone can get you out of there on bail—"

"I don't need a fucking lawyer!"

That part I'd said too loud. Kearney was staring at me. Ramirez was moving in.

"I'm sorry, Cèsar," Suzy said again. I was real sick of hearing those words. I didn't think I could hear them again without losing it.

The police station was so loud, so crowded. I was trapped in a sea of desks and concrete walls. Erin was still reaching for me with her cracked manicure, gazing at my ceiling with a look of postmortem horror, and I could smell that meaty scent of blood.

I didn't even feel it when Ramirez took the

phone from me and hung it up.

The Office of Preternatural Affairs thought I was guilty and they were shaking me loose before I dragged them down with me.

I was on my own.

The holding cell was a temporary thing. Wouldn't be long at all before I got face time in front of a judge and found myself in real deep shit—an actual jail, not a room with bars in the back of a police station.

I still wasn't worried about being found guilty. I hadn't killed Erin and the evidence would prove it. It wasn't my Glock on the table—it wouldn't even have my fingerprints on it. Plus, there were security cameras around the apartment complex.

We would find out that someone had come home with us. It would prove that I had struggled with the attacker, making the wreckage in my living room and kitchen. And then they would be able to prove that the attacker had knocked me out and shot Erin.

It was the only story that made sense. The only possible explanation.

But they would determine all of that after I'd been in jail for months. After I'd had a lawyer assigned to me and been dragged over the coals in a long trial.

By that time, my life would already be ruined. The killer long gone.

It wouldn't be any justice for Erin.

No, I wasn't going on trial. I wasn't following

the Bloody Douchebag Gang into prison. It wasn't happening.

Someone had messed with Erin—had messed with *me*—and I was going to find out who.

That was the decision I'd come to after five minutes of pacing in the holding cell. It only took a split second after that to decide how I'd escape.

You see, I'd been able to escape this whole time. But Suzy had asked me to cooperate, so I had been cooperating. Why not? Someone had been going to save me anyway.

But since the OPA thought I was guilty too, there was no point in sticking around. There was only one person that could prove my innocence, and that guy was me. I wouldn't be able to do it if I was stuck behind bars.

I climbed up on the bench. It had been bolted to the wall so that it couldn't be used as a weapon. It wasn't directly below the narrow barred window, but it was only a foot or two to the right, and I could reach it. I had long arms. And not just long—but muscular.

Three days a week at the gym hadn't built me up like a bear. I mostly went to do the cardio machines. A few hours on the treadmill to help make sure that I could catch a suspect on foot.

What had given me these insane shoulders were the foul-tasting poultices that I chewed every morning, the potions brewed on my stovetop in Walmart cookware, and the charms I kept hidden in my gun safe.

I wasn't a normal human. Not like these cops were, and not like the people they usually arrested were.

They weren't ready for someone like me.

My hands tightened on the bars. My forearms flexed and the muscles bulged like steel cable under the skin. The scratches from wrist to elbow twisted and distorted. Magic surged in my veins.

Crunch.

I was holding the window in my hands. Pulled it free of the brick, steel frame and all. I dropped it to the bench and didn't look behind me. I knew the cops were coming—that hadn't been a quiet noise. I could hear them shouting, and I had about three seconds before someone freaked out and shot me in the back.

Hauling myself into the window frame, I wriggled my shoulders through. They almost got stuck, like a snake that had eaten a mouse too big for its maw. But once I had that part out, the rest of me was no problem. It was an easy drop to the ground outside.

I was in a parking lot. It was raining hard. There were police cruisers around—a lot of police cruisers. The fence was twice my height and topped with barbed wire.

It only took a second for a skull-shattering alarm to go off.

Jesus, my hangover wasn't loving that.

Three long strides and I'd reached the fence. Dug my fingers into the chain-link, found a toehold, started climbing. Domingo would be proud to see how fast I moved.

At the joint where the fence formed a right angle, there were two posts right next to each other without barbed wire on top. Good handholds. Nothing sharp that could cut me open.

I leveraged myself over the top and dropped onto the street.

The alarm had gone off quickly, but the men who were following me were slow, sluggish humans, unprepared for a magically juiced witch on the run. I wondered what they thought of what they saw—how quickly I had crossed the parking lot and scaled the fence, how little the fall to the other side had fazed me. I wonder if they might have been thinking that something supernatural had been going on or if they just thought I was on speed or something.

Denial was a hell of a drug.

Either way, I was out of there in a heartbeat.

CHAPTER SIX

THERE WAS NOTHING FREE about being a man on the run. Hurtling through the streets, bolting down alleys to avoid cop cars, hiding behind Dumpsters that smelled like year-old milk—it was about as free as being in the holding cell with the Sureños.

But eventually the sirens faded. I was alone by midnight.

For now, alone would have to be as good as free.

It was rainy and cold. Shelter was gonna be priority soon, but my picture was out there and I needed to be careful where my face showed up. That meant no hotels.

There were other places I could comfortably disappear. Helltown was probably a relatively safe place to hide from the LAPD, and if I was feeling real bold I could even head to the undercity. Because the demons down below would *never* fuck with an OPA agent, right?

Little bit of sarcastic humor there, in case you didn't catch it.

But I didn't go to Helltown. I'd been running without a plan so my feet had taken charge, directing me back to my apartment. It was the only place I could think to start.

Seeing my apartment building rise out of the darkness didn't give me the relieved feeling it usually did. None of that "the day is over, now I can chill in front of my *Firefly* DVDs for the seventeenth time" warmth. I was detached. This wasn't my place; it was the scene of a crime.

I sat in the bushes across the street for an hour, waiting to see if anyone was coming or going, but didn't spot a single cop. I didn't see any unmarked black SUVs, either—dead giveaway for the Union.

How many hours had it been since the police hit my front door? Sixteen? No way they'd cleared the scene that fast.

But I didn't see anyone, and I couldn't question the why. Once the OPA caught wind of my disappearance, they would be back to look for me, and getting caught at my apartment would be a fast and embarrassing end to my night as a fugitive.

I was up the fire escape about as fast as I'd gotten up the chain link fence. The ladder hadn't been lowered, but I was still juiced on magic and a ten-foot jump was easy for me. Then it was just a matter of going up seven stories and finding my window. I tried to pull out the screen without making a sound.

It felt like I was sneaking back into Pops's house after a night out with Domingo again, except I didn't have my brother's jokes to keep the mood light.

My apartment's furnishings were colorless in the dark. I stopped by the window and listened for any sign of investigators lingering in my apartment. I could hear the guy upstairs working out, like he always did at one in the morning. No better time to lift weights and grunt loudly, right? At least I had the tact to save it for the afternoons.

But he was upstairs, and there were no cops in my place. Didn't mean they couldn't sneak up on me. Had to go fast.

I'd lived in the apartment for as long as I'd worked with the OPA—two years. It wasn't anything fancy, but it was the first place that I'd lived without Pops breathing down my neck, so it was mine. Those movie posters on the wall? The Blu-ray collection? All the Brandon Sanderson books? *Mine*. And it felt like a major violation to have that stuff taped and tagged. Bet you anything that they'd photographed everything, too. Even my damn underwear drawer.

Judging by the blood on my hallway carpet, the crime scene hadn't been scrubbed yet. Guess they would probably leave that to the landlord so that he'd have to pay the cleaning bill, too. I didn't really want to know if Erin was still there, but I checked—bathtub was empty. The blood smear was just the way I'd left it, but there was a clear spot where her body used to be.

Didn't look real in the dark. Black blood, white floor. Looked like crime scene photos.

Yeah. A crime scene photo. I could keep detached.

What would I have been looking for if this had been an investigation?

I headed into my living room and looked around. Suspect was obviously a social recluse. Spent too much money on movies—definitely didn't have a girlfriend. Had been three years since the last girlfriend, actually, which was something I acknowledged with a pang of annoyance. And none of that information helped me figure out who could have actually killed Erin Karwell.

Ah, hell, I couldn't keep detached here. Not in my place.

Better get what I'd come for and leave.

They'd collected a lot of the objects in my living room for evidence, but the gun safe was bolted to the floor. It hadn't budged.

I opened my gun safe by passing my hand over the handle. Magic flared and a lock clicked inside. The door swung open.

There was one gun in my gun safe, and I kept it there unless I was doing fieldwork. It was a Desert Eagle that Fritz had given me for my birthday. It wasn't required for OPA agents to pack heat, so it was the first firearm I'd ever owned. I hated that thing. Felt like carrying it around meant I was expecting to shoot something, and I didn't do that.

But I grabbed it, along with the belt. If someone was out to frame me for murder, I had better be ready to defend myself.

The Desert Eagle was the only weapon in there. Most of the space was taken up by trophies from resolved investigations. I had gris-gris, charms, potions, photographs, even one of Black Jack's tarot cards. Call it research. In that theoretical "someday" where free time and motivation intersected, I wanted to figure out how to deconstruct the spells cast by the OPA's Most Wanted and put them to practical use. For now, it was basically a big box of useless crap.

The drawer at the bottom of the safe, however, was filled with dozens of Steno pads' worth of personal notes. I took those. If the OPA cracked my safe, they would put them into storage and I'd never get them back. Their warehouses were worse than the ones in *Indiana Jones*; once something went in, it never came out.

There was one active case file in there, too. I'd locked it up before heading to The Olive Pit the night before.

This new case was supposed to be my reward for taking care of Black Jack so quickly. An easy bag-and-tag. The suspect was named Isobel Stonecrow—possibly a necromancer, probably a fake—and she had been earning money by claiming that she could connect them with their dead loved ones. If she was a mundane human having fun, she would be shocked when the actual witches showed up at her door. And if she was the real McCoy, we had even more unpleasant surprises in store for her.

I took that file, too. Might as well. Hopefully I'd be getting back to work soon anyway.

After that, it was a matter of getting dressed in comfortable clothes again. Jeans, a black tee, my favorite leather jacket. The inner pockets could hold my notebooks easily. I threaded my belt through the Desert Eagle's holster and wore it on my hip.

I was pulling the window screen down again when I heard the lock on the front door click.

I froze halfway out of the window, one foot on the fire escape and the other on the carpet. My hand went to my hip but my brain stopped working.

My visitors were probably the cops or the Union—neither of whom I wanted seeing me here—and that meant I should probably run. But there was a small chance that it was whoever had killed Erin coming back to look at his handiwork. Witches would do that sometimes. Go back to where they performed a ritual, clean up their residual energy, collect supplies. Made it easy to catch them.

In the time it took me to realize there was a decision to make, the door opened. A small shape slipped into my living room.

It was Suzy. Ah, Suzy. She was obviously working because she was wearing professional attire. Tailored black suit, white shirt, black necktie. It was meant to make us all look uniform, but there was no hiding the waspish waist and incredible legs underneath the comfortable cotton. Even with her hair up, you could tell she was beautiful.

She looked shocked to see me. Her hand was already in her jacket, reaching for her shoulder rig.

"Oh, Cèsar," she said. "You idiot."

She wasn't wrong.

There were people moving behind her. I couldn't tell who, but she wasn't alone. That made the decision for me.

WITCH HUNT

I was out the window, over the side of the fire escape. Flying. Falling.

As soon as I hit, I was running again.

CHAPTER SEVEN

THE OLIVE PIT WAS a mix of old and new, hip and nostalgic. The first floor had wood paneling and leather furniture. The second-floor balcony, on the other hand, was all acrylic—you could look through it to see the classier decorations below.

When it was running hot on a Friday or Saturday, they would get the spotlights going, and the transparent floor and chandeliers looked insane. But when I reached The Pit after fleeing from my apartment, it was quiet. You didn't even notice the second floor with the lights off. It just looked like a cigar bar or something. Glistening wood floors, shelves of old books, outdated maps on the walls. The kind of place you could kick back with a martini and a cigar for hours of bullshit with the guys.

On a Wednesday night—or Thursday morning, take your pick—there was nobody there but the staff. One of the girls was leaning on the handle of her mop like she wouldn't be able to stand without it. Mascara striped her cheeks.

I didn't know her name. I'd only ever paid any

attention to Erin. I wished I knew her name, wished I knew her well enough to tell her how sorry I was. Hated seeing girls cry.

Shaking the rain off my lapels, I headed in.

The waitress noticed that I was approaching and fixed a polite smile to her face. "We're closing." Didn't even sound like she'd been crying. Good at covering up.

"I know. I'm here to talk with you."

Her cheeks went pale. She ran a hand over the curls trimmed short to her scalp. "Is this about Erin?" She knew what was up. I probably wasn't the first one here to talk about her. Luckily, she didn't recognize me.

"Did you know her well?" I asked, extracting one of the Steno pads from my jacket. The most recent one was only half filled. I found the line that said "Black Jack got nailed," skipped to the next blank page, and wrote "The Olive Pit" at the top.

"Guess so," she said. She rested her cheek on her hands, wrapped around the mop, and gave me a scrutinizing look. Like she was trying to decide if she recognized me.

"Erin was in trouble. She came in last night with a black eye."

"Did she?"

"Yeah, right eye." I pointed at mine to illustrate. "Had you seen her with signs of abuse before?"

"No, she wasn't abused. Not Erin. She's not that kind of woman." Her throat worked as she swallowed. "She *wasn't* that kind of woman."

"What kind of woman was she?"

"Smart. She always knew what she wanted and

stood up for it. She worked hard. She took all the extra shifts without complaining."

Yeah, Erin had looked like a smart girl to me. I believed it. And I wrote that down, too. It felt important to make note of what was good about her, the things that had marked her as special when she had still been breathing. "Was she hard up for money?"

"I guess so, but who isn't these days?" The waitress pointed at the bar with her mop handle. The half-light from the lamps highlighted red on her high cheekbones, the bare curves of her shoulders. "Nobody worked the bar like she did. She was very dedicated to her job, and she got tipped like nobody else because she was such a delight to spend time with. If she was here just for the money, then she faked it well."

"So you don't think that she was abused," I said.

"Not a chance. She wouldn't have put up with it."

"Did you ever spend time together outside of work?"

"I work three jobs, brother," the waitress said. "The only thing I see outside of work is my pillow."

I laughed at that. It felt good to laugh. Made my face ache a little, but the weight in my chest lightened a few ounces.

I only realized that the front door had opened again because I could hear the patter of rain on the sidewalk outside. Then the waitress's eyes focused behind me. She stepped back, propped her mop against the bar, disappeared into the kitchen. She was fast. I'd barely reached for her and opened my mouth to ask her to stop before she was gone.

And then something hard pressed into the small of my back.

"Freeze, a-hole," said a woman behind me. "Your nuts are mine."

The moment of paralyzing fear instantly melted away. There was only one woman that obsessed with anything below my belt, and unfortunately all she wanted to do was chew it up and spit it out.

"Suzy," I sighed. She let me turn around. She didn't have a gun—she had jammed the hilt of a folding knife into my back. I lifted my hands to my shoulders in a gesture of surrender and arched my eyebrows in a gesture of, *Are you kidding me?*

Even if she was serious, there was nothing intimidating about a five-foot-tall woman. My reach was at least twice hers. I could have knocked her out before she got close enough to stab me. Not that I would have ever knocked Suzy out, mind you—but I *could* have.

I liked to think that we were friends. She knew I could overpower her. She also knew I wouldn't.

Suzy rolled her eyes and flicked her knife shut. "You're a dumbass."

"About so many things, yeah, but why now?"

"Because I found you here. *Here*, Cèsar? Really? You might as well walk through the front doors of the Union offices with a sign that says 'I'm guilty' taped to your shirt."

"You followed me," I guessed.

"No, you're pretty slick on the streets. We lost you two blocks north of your apartment. But I know you. I know what you're doing. It wasn't hard to guess you'd come here looking for answers."

"And yet you came alone."

"Guess I'm a dumbass too." She shrugged. "You're trying to prove your innocence, aren't you?"

"Of course I am. But I don't need to prove anything to you, right? You know that I didn't kill Erin Karwell." It seemed ridiculous that I even had to say it. Suzy should have known it. *Everyone* should've known.

There was sympathy in her big brown eyes. "Then who's the culprit?"

"That's the problem—I don't know. I don't even remember leaving the bar last night. I guess I drank too much, and then I woke up to find everything like…well, you saw it."

Suzy's lips pinched into a thin line. Was she thinking that meant I was guilty?

"Look, Suze, there's no way I did it, and you know it," I said.

"Well," she said, "let's finish what you're here to do."

She yanked the badge off of her belt and marched for the door to the kitchen. I was only a few steps behind her.

There were two women in back. They were standing beside the door to one of those big walk-in freezers. The schedule was on the wall behind them—including Erin's name signed with a smiley heart—and shelves of alcohol to the left.

The waitress that I'd spoken to earlier looked

alarmed to see me. Her body language was totally different, like a hamster about to bolt for cover. She was hiding behind her coworker even though the second waitress was six inches shorter.

Suzy brandished her badge. "Agent Takeuchi, Federal Bureau of Investigation."

"I know who you are," said the waitress in front. "You come here all the time with all of *those* guys." She didn't sound fond of our coworkers. Bet it was because government employees were too poor to tip well.

"What's your name, ma'am?" Suzy asked.

"Thandy Cannon. Second shift manager." She waved over her shoulder at the other woman. "This is Ladasha."

"Okay, Thandy and Ladasha. I'm investigating the murder of one of your coworkers—Erin Karwell. I need anything you can give me. Whom she might have talked to last night, whom she was dating, friends and family. People with a grudge."

"Oh yeah?" Thandy asked with a sneer. "You need to know who she was dating, do you?"

"This isn't girl talk or gossip," Suzy said. "This is an official investigation."

"Is that why you're dragging her boyfriend around?"

It took me a second to realize that Thandy was talking about me.

Suzy shot me a questioning look and I shook my head. No way. I was not dating Erin. Of course, that had been despite my best efforts, but Suzy didn't need to know how roundly Erin had turned me down. My pride was already having a terrible day.

"You recognize this man?" Suzy asked, jerking a thumb at me.

"Hell yeah I do," said Thandy. "That's the asshole that yelled at Erin for twenty minutes before dragging her out of here last night. That's the guy who killed her."

CHAPTER EIGHT

SUZY WAS GOOD AT her job in a different way than I was. She was a witch, too, a jack of all trades. But that wasn't what made her effective. It was the fact she would do anything to clean up a mess.

Today, that "anything" was bribery.

She was smooth. She made a few benjamins appear from her wallet and Thandy and Ladasha promised not to talk about what they'd seen, quick as you please.

That money made the waitresses sign the standard nondisclosure agreement. The paper flashed with magic when Suzy tucked it back in her jacket. Thandy and Ladasha wouldn't be able to say a thing about seeing me leave with Erin, even if they wanted to—the curse would choke them when they tried to speak. A pretty piece of magic from the OPA's very best witches.

I was still numb with anger when Suzy took me home. I didn't even realize she'd taken me back to her place until we were already there.

"You shouldn't," I said as she parked in front of her townhouse. "You'll get in trouble if you're seen with me."

She punched the remote and her garage door lifted. "What else are you going to do if I don't give you somewhere to sleep, huh? Go to your apartment and curl up in bed, wait for someone to find you? Use your ID to check in at a strip motel?"

"I'm not that stupid."

"You could have had me fooled." She pulled into the garage. "Get your ass inside, Hawke."

Her townhouse was a cozy two-story wedged between a pair of identical units. The HOA kept a tight grip on exterior decorations, so from the outside, there was no telling them apart. She had the same blinds that the others did. Her lawn was maintained by the same service. Only difference was, her front door was painted bright blue. And once you walked through that door, the whole world changed.

Suzy's townhouse was bigger on the inside—more like a Victorian mansion than a barebones townhouse. I'd measured it inside and outside once. One living room wall to the other was sixty feet across. But if you stepped out and measured the space between her neighboring townhouses, it was barely thirty feet wide. Don't ask where that extra square footage came from. I was pretty sure even Suzy didn't know how it worked.

She packed that extra space with enough ingredients and crystals to supply three covens, making her townhouse the magical equivalent of a hurricane. The amount of mystical energy swirling in her house was even crazier than Suzy herself.

Technically, dimensional distortions were

against the law. Not to mention that she probably would have given the HOA board an embolism if they realized what she was doing to the neighborhood's metaphysics. Luckily for Suzy, the HOA board didn't include any witches—but the OPA did. We caught her as soon as she finished casting the spell. Her wards weren't good enough to hide what she'd done from us.

But this was Suzy. An agent had shown up to arrest her and she'd ended up with a job offer instead.

She'd been hired a month after me. We had shared a cubicle ever since. And she still had her crazy-ass townhouse two years later.

The room flexed around me as I stepped through her doorway. I had to duck under dried herbs and step over a cat to get inside. "Bad kitty," Suzy said, scooping up her cat in one arm before he could escape between my legs. He had a big gold bell hanging from his neck that glinted red out the corner of my eye. Some kind of protection spell.

"New familiar?" I didn't recognize this particular cat. Not that I'd been to Suzy's place since she'd bought new furniture last year. I'd helped her carry some couches upstairs as a favor. When you were as big as I was, you were always the first one to get called when someone needed heavy crap moved.

"Witches of my ilk don't have familiars. We have sacrifices. Cat is not one of them."

"Cat? That's his name?"

"I'm not a poetic soul," she said, tossing her jacket on the hook, fluffing out her hair, and heading into the living room.

Her living room was filled with smoke from smoldering incense cones. Every shelf was covered in crystals and she had herbs drying in every window. There was a permanent altar where most people would have a TV. Her assortment of deity figures could put a museum to shame—Horned God and Mother Goddess, a weeping Buddha, a crucifix with a tiny Jesus in the middle. Ready for any ritual at any time.

The smell of rose and jasmine made me sneeze twice, hard. It wasn't just the incense. I was sensitive to magical energy—the stronger the active spell, the stronger my allergy attack. It was pretty much the most embarrassing quirk for a witch to have.

"I'm gonna open a window," I said, scrubbing my nose furiously.

"Do it and die." She breezed past me and climbed the stairs. "The couch is yours for the night, but we'll need to figure out what you're doing tomorrow."

"Proving my innocence," I called up after her. It was hard to work up conviction when another sneezing fit caught me.

I eyeballed her windows, trying to decide which I could crack without her noticing, and realized that one of them was covered in plywood. *Broken?*

I didn't even see the clothing hurtling at me from the top of the stairs until I'd been smacked in the face. I caught them on my chest, picked them apart. They were a t-shirt and sweats that looked awfully familiar. Suzy yelled down at me, "I got those out of your locker at work. Don't sit on my couch with your muddy clothes."

I changed in the downstairs bathroom with Cat's cold, appraising gaze behind me in the mirror. The bathroom mirror was shattered on the right side. It fragmented my face into five frowning sections. I wasn't looking good—I could have passed for something dredged out of Helltown.

I tossed my clothes over an empty towel rack to dry then splashed water on my face and the back of my neck.

Even Suzy's bathroom was filled with crystals and knickknacks. A row of porcelain cats with right paws uplifted filled the shelf across from her toilet. If Cat weren't so damn furry, he'd be indistinguishable from his china counterparts.

Once I was as clean I was going to get, I dropped onto Suzy's living room couch. I felt like I could have passed out the instant I settled onto the beaten furniture. The alcohol hangover had faded hours ago, but I had a shock hangover, too. The throbbing ache of a life turned upside down. Wasn't that long ago that I'd squirmed out a police station window.

Suzy's voice drifted downstairs. "There's leftover chicken in the refrigerator if you're hungry."

Sounded good to me, but the fridge was around the corner about ten feet away, and it sounded like too much work. I kicked my feet up and sank against the arm of the sofa.

The pipes in the walls groaned as the shower

started.

My eyes traveled to the folder I had dropped on Suzy's coffee table. The red tab labeled "Isobel Stonecrow" and a ten-digit code specific to her case. I pulled it into my lap, flipped open the cover, and skimmed the details again.

This Stonecrow was some kind of witch who could talk to spirits. It was a rare talent, but not impossible. We used to have a witch on retainer at the OPA that did something like that. He would touch skulls and tell you what the victim was thinking before she died. Useful guy to have around. Made it real easy to close cases that the mundane police thought had gone cold.

He'd killed himself last year. We hadn't found another witch that could talk to the dead since then.

But this Isobel Stonecrow, she might be able to do the same thing.

She might be able to ask Erin who killed her.

Stonecrow's case file was a hell of a lot more interesting with that thought on the tip of my brain. I started reading it again with new eyes.

Three different families had filed complaints about her this year. One in Long Beach, one up near Sacramento, another down in San Jose. She sure got around. Wonder why she was traveling all over the state like that. Trying to keep us off her tail?

Those complaints hadn't inspired this investigation. The last of those had come in three months ago, and we usually acted on real problems faster than that. If it wasn't a problem *now*, it wasn't a problem at all.

But the overview letter said that they wanted Stonecrow nailed within the week, and the budget set out for grabbing her was a lot more than we usually give one obnoxious witch.

That told me two things: first, that Stonecrow must have pissed someone off at the OPA, and second, that I wouldn't be the only one looking for her. This wasn't a case that was going to wait until I get back. They would have already given it to one of the other guys. Who knows? Maybe they were already on her trail tonight.

Not good.

I heard Suzy come down the stairs as I studied the files. Her shadow slid over me, doubled and tripled in size by all the candlelight. Her silhouette was almost as big as her personality. "Did you warm up the chicken?" she asked as she stepped into the kitchen. I smelled her body wash as she passed. She had used peach soap. Smelled feminine, like soft skin and curves.

And magical incense.

I sneezed again.

"No, I didn't get that far." My voice was embarrassingly stuffy. Couldn't breathe through my nose anymore. "I'm not hungry."

Suzy muttered some choice insults about all my favorite body parts and slammed around in the kitchen. She also said something about "stupid men."

I snorted and kept reading.

Isobel Stonecrow didn't have an address. She'd never had an address, in fact. No place of employment. No medical history. No Social

Security number. No coven affiliations. If it hadn't been for three furious families short a wad of cash, we wouldn't have even known she existed. So her name was probably a pseudonym. If I could find her real name, I could find where she lived—if she lived anywhere at all.

With wandering feet like that, maybe she was mobile. Sleeping in the backseat of a car or something.

The information in the files was limited, but there might've been more in the OPA database. Witness testimony, for instance.

"Hey Suzy," I called, marking a few notes in the margins, "you got any—"

I looked up and forgot all my words.

For a tough little pixie of a woman, Suzy's legs looked awfully long when they were bare. It took me a few long seconds to get from her bare, dainty feet to the swell of her thighs and to realize that she was wearing a nightgown that didn't cover much of anything. If she walked too fast, she would flash panties.

Her charcoal hair was loose around her shoulders and she was holding two bowls of food. Like every man's wet dream.

"Uh, broken," I said. That didn't make any sense. Shit. "Your window's broken. So's your mirror." That wasn't what I'd meant to talk about. It wasn't even what I had been thinking about.

She set the bowls down. "Some dick broke in while I was at work two days ago and stole a few things. This neighborhood's going downhill fast. But you get why I didn't want you opening a window now, right?" She stepped into the kitchen again.

Yeah, I got it. The thought of Suzy living alone in a neighborhood like this was enough to get my guts twisting. "Because you're afraid of being attacked again."

"No, because I've cursed my windows." She smiled devilishly at me as she set a pair of plates on the coffee table. "Next bastard that touches them is going to have more boils than a sailor's prick. Rice?" I didn't say yes, but she spooned some onto my plate anyway, topping it with chicken that smelled citrusy. "Eat it, Hawke. You look like you're about to pass out."

She was eating with chopsticks like she was born with them attached to her hands, but she'd brought me a fork. Bless her.

My appetite returned the instant the chicken touched my tongue. I gave a low groan. "That's good stuff."

Suzy grinned. "Yeah, it is." She was sitting on the coffee table, not the other couch. Her bare knees brushed against mine.

Jesus, that was distracting. She was *never* this distracting in our cubicle.

"What's that?" Suzy pointed at the Stonecrow folder.

"Oh. Uh." I rubbed the back of my neck and tried not to look at her legs. *Don't look at her legs, Hawke.* "It was the last case assigned to me before… It was assigned yesterday. It's for this witch, some flavor of necromancer, who might be talking to the dead. I thought that I could get her to talk to Erin and find out what happened."

"I don't think that's a good idea. You need to get out of town, and fast."

"What, and give up my job, my family, my life?" *My collection of special edition* Star Wars *DVDs?*

"The OPA's not going to give you any help with this case, Cèsar. It looks bad. Really bad. Worse, it doesn't look like anything infernal or magical. They're prepared to let you go through the mundane court system."

"I can't believe Fritz is letting that fly," I said. Fritz loved me. At least, I thought he did.

"Even Friederling has bosses." She sighed. "Look, I'll do what I can about the case while you're gone. But for now you need to get away from Los Angeles, and you need to do it before the OPA decides that they should have a witch tag you with a tracking spell."

I would've liked to see them try. I might not have been doubling the size of my apartment with magic, but I could detect and blast away passive spells like that in my sleep. "There had to be someone else in the apartment with Erin and me. That means there's evidence. A trail I can follow. If I leave, that trail goes cold."

"And if you don't leave, you get to go to prison."

I wanted to point out how they could only send me to prison if I was proven guilty, and they needed evidence for that, too. But what if Erin's cause of death really had been magical or infernal? The fact the OPA wasn't investigating meant that there weren't any witches or demon hunters to sweep for evidence. The LAPD's detectives were good at what they did—when it came to humans. But they didn't have the tools they needed for this.

Suzy wouldn't hear reason, though. I knew what it sounded like when she had made up her mind.

I'd been pushing the same piece of chicken around my plate for a few minutes without eating. I made myself take a last bite. "I'm exhausted."

A sympathetic look. "Yeah, I bet you are. Catch a few hours of sleep. I'll hook you up with a bus ticket before I go to work tomorrow."

Suzy finished eating and cleaned up, which involved bending over a few times. I tried not to notice.

Damn.

She gave me some blankets and dimmed the lights. "I'll wake you up at four. You need anything?"

I told her I didn't. My resolve vanished in a puff of incense smoke when she headed upstairs, and I craned my neck to watch the globes of her ass flexing under her panties as she climbed. *Double damn. Triple damn. Damnation above and below and everywhere in between.*

I waited until I heard her door close before finding her laptop.

We all had them. The OPA issued laptops to its employees so we could take our work everywhere we went. No rest for salaried government employees, right? I usually left mine docked in its workstation, but Suzy was a workaholic. I knew it had to be around somewhere.

As I suspected, I found Cat sitting on her machine in the entryway. He gave me an offended look when I tugged it out from underneath his furry butt.

Our passwords needed to be changed every quarter, but Suzy's password was always easy to figure out. She mixed up the ingredients that she kept in jars on her desk—always the same ingredients in a different order. Lotus, dragon's blood, thyme, jasmine, moonstone. Not that I'd been watching her type or anything.

Anyway, it took three tries to get the order right, and I was logged in.

A quick search of the database brought up witness testimonies for Isobel Stonecrow, just as I'd been hoping. I printed them out. Stuffed them in my jacket. Put Suzy's laptop back where I found it.

I spent a full minute at the base of her stairs and thought about leaving while she was asleep. But someone had broken into Suzy's house. If I hit the streets tonight, I would spend the whole time stressing about her all vulnerable in bed, tangled up in sheets that smelled like her peach body wash, wondering if she would look like Erin in the morning.

I needed sleep. There was no avoiding that. Might as well do it where I could keep Suzy safe.

The blankets she'd given me smelled like Cat. I wrapped up in them and closed my eyes.

I was unconscious before my head hit the arm of the sofa.

CHAPTER NINE

I DREAMED OF ERIN.

We were tangled in each other, her hips rocking, my hands mounding the twin swells of her ass. She was grinding, groaning. Her head rolled back on her shoulders. Her chest was freckled. I licked the sweat from between her breasts and bit her nipple. She liked that—judging by the sounds, she *really* liked that.

We moved in tandem, the two of us. Bodies slamming against the cabinets. Hands clutching at the counter. She was close to her peak. Her arm flailed and knocked the toaster onto the floor.

There was something wrong here—something missing between us. Something I had forgotten.

Couldn't stop. Couldn't think.

There was nothing but our bodies and the hunger.

She came hard, screaming. Her fingernails dug into my pecs. Even that knifelike pain was pleasure, carrying me toward the edge with her. I was balls deep, about to shoot a load inside this gorgeous woman, and I didn't care that my heart had stopped beating.

But I knew I was about to die.

I shocked awake with a weight pressing on my chest. For a half second, I thought that I'd been buried alive. It was dark. I couldn't breathe.

Then I saw two pale circles staring at me and realized that I wasn't in a grave—I just had Cat smothering me. He was purring like a jackhammer and kneading Suzy's blankets under his polydactyl paws. His whiskers tickled against my chin.

I pushed the cat off, let the sheets fall, pressed a fist to my chest. Heart was slamming against my breastbone. It wasn't hot, but I was drenched in sweat.

Needed to breathe. Could have used another poultice for strength, too.

I raked my hands through my sweaty hair, leaned on my knees. I was all right. I was still here, even if Erin wasn't. There was still time to get justice for her. All I needed was the manila folder on Suzy's coffee table and some time. I checked the clock on the wall. Bad news was, Cat had only allowed me to sleep for two hours, and my eyeballs felt drier than granite and everything still hurt from yesterday. Good news was that Suzy was still asleep.

I got dressed, donned my jacket, and was almost ready to go when I saw the phone light up on the table near the sofa.

It was Suzy's work phone.

Ignoring my whispering conscience, I flipped it open. It was from the OPA, not a boyfriend. She had gotten a standard tracker text—an alert telling her that a suspect in her current case had been sighted. It contained a series of digits that would translate to coordinates once decoded. I scribbled the number in my notebook before deleting the message from her phone.

The first four digits attached to the code were the same as the serial number on my manila folder. It proved what I already suspected: someone else *had* been given the Stonecrow case.

And that someone was Suzy.

What the hell? I'd told her that I wanted to talk to this Stonecrow witch, and she'd just told me to blow town. Suzy should have told me that she had the inside track on locating Stonecrow. On the bright side, now I wasn't going to have to search very hard to find Stonecrow. The morning was already looking up.

I gave Cat a rub, got out the door.

The witch wasn't going to catch herself.

Working for the OPA, you don't get out on your own until you've already been walked around a few times on a short leash. Aside from the mandatory ride-along every agent has to do with the Union, there's also a six-month probationary period where you get all the baby cases: kids slaughtering the pet cat to try to raise the dead, snake oil salesmen, housewives trying to emulate spells on *Charmed* and accidentally summoning demons. All the stuff that has no malicious intent and no victim but still has to get cleaned up.

Shady Groves Cemetery was the number one

site of these bullshit cases. It was right next to a high school on the outskirts of the city, so that was where most complaints of lurking "Satanists" (emo teenagers without enough extracurriculars) got reported.

I'd been on so many somnolent stakeouts at Shady Groves that I had the layout memorized. It was up on a hill. Parking lot on the south side, school on the west side, bodies all up under the trees. The mausoleums and Victorian-era statues are the real tourist draw. The place has more creepy buildings than a small town in Louisiana.

If Stonecrow was the real deal, then she wasn't a big player. Because that was where the tracker text was sending me: Shady Groves Cemetery. The little leagues. Training wheels for people who want to be necromancers.

So I didn't bother preparing before heading over. I didn't borrow Suzy's kitchen to brew a magic neutralization potion. I didn't get ropes or other restraints. I did take the gun—figured that'd keep my ass covered well enough if Stonecrow turned out to be hostile. I might even be able to shoot someone with it if they stood still long enough for me to get my bearings.

In retrospect, it wasn't one of my best plans. Mostly because I had no plan at all.

I hit Shady Groves Cemetery about an hour before dawn. Even at four in the morning, Los Angeles traffic blows monkey balls. It was stop and go the entire way—mostly stop.

Eventually, Shady Groves came out of the predawn gloom. I didn't park the stolen Toyota in the parking lot, since it would be visible from the graves. I took it up a frontage road around back. The tires thumped along for a couple hundred yards, bouncing me around like dice in a cup.

I could have picked a better car to steal. As in, maybe one with any suspension whatsoever.

Then I heard a *thump* and a *hiss*, the Toyota sagged on one side, and suspension was suddenly the least of my problems.

"Of course," I muttered, killing the engine and getting out to look, even though I already knew what I was going to see. I'd blown a tire on a sharp rock that had been invisible in the darkness. Guess that was just my luck that week.

I kicked the tire. My short, illicit affair with the Tercel was over.

I found my way through the bushes to a section of chain-link that had been cut away long before I ever started working with the OPA. It was probably one of my trainee predecessors that did it; all of us have been through Shady Groves during our probationary periods, and I can think of at least one or two fat-assed agents that would have gotten sick of having to climb.

Pushing through the bushes, I beat away the snarls of metal and stumbled into the cemetery.

The second I freed my jacket, I realized that I should have taken at least a few seconds to prepare before going after Stonecrow.

Mostly because I was suddenly suffocating.

I'm not much into big showy rituals, but I know what it feels like when someone else is doing one. The air goes thick with magic and it's like trying to breathe underwater. That was what happened to me when I crossed over the invisible line of wards underneath the trees rimming Shady Groves. My chest clenched up, throat closed, eyes watering.

I sneezed into the elbow of my sleeve. And then sneezed again, and again.

Shit. If I'd been on another OPA training run, I would have gotten so many points off on covert ops. Needed to clear my head. And my nose.

Necromancer or not, Stonecrow had real power. But I left my gun in my holster as I crouch-walked through the bushes, trying to make as little noise as possible for a six-foot-tall ape like myself. I plastered my back to the edge of a mausoleum and blew a few more muffled sneezes into my sleeve.

When I finally got control of my breathing, I heard the drums.

The rhythm immediately made me think of tribal things. The jungles of Central America. Wildcats and parrots. Those big bass drums that you pound with mallets before battle and make your enemies shit themselves because it sounds so badass.

The drumming was punctuated by a dry jangling noise. Not metal, but maybe wood.

A thickly accented voice echoed over the graveyard.

"By the light of the coyote moon, I summon the spirits," she said. "By the dirt of these hallowed graves, I summon the spirits." More rattling, another beat on the drums.

That accent didn't sound like anything I'd heard before. I could barely understand a damn thing she was saying. But between what I did understand and the overwhelming sting of her magic, I knew that I'd found the suspect.

I peered around the edge of the mausoleum. Further down the hill, I glimpsed faint, flickering candlelight reflecting off of smooth brown skin. *Bare* skin, to be exact.

A woman was standing in front of a grave with her arms raised. Bone bracelets encircled her wrists. That was the only thing she seemed to be wearing above the waist, aside from a feathered headdress that had probably required the death of an entire endangered species to produce. There was some serious meat on those half-naked hips. The swell of her ass was covered in a strip of coyote pelt.

Beyond her shoulder, I could make out a pair of terrified-looking faces. They were far beyond the light from her fire. The candles lit their eyes with bright pinpricks. It was enough to tell that they were both wearing suits, like they'd be off to office jobs once they were done with the graveyard girl.

So this would be Isobel Stonecrow and her latest clients.

She was still talking in that thick, obscure accent. "Gods of the sky and stars! Deliver to me Brad Stewart!"

"Brian," said the woman in the suit skirt. "His name was Brian."

A pause, and Stonecrow called, "*Brian!*"

I sneezed repeatedly into my sleeve, trying to smother my face with my suit so that nobody would hear. The magic was too much for me. I slid to the ground with my arms over my nose and mouth, sitting on muddy grass that was still wet from yesterday's rain.

Fortunately, Stonecrow was drumming again, even louder than before. She beat that damn drum until it sounded like the skin might break.

Then, suddenly, she stopped.

"Cindy?" Her voice sounded different, higher-pitched and with an American accent. "What are you doing here, Cindy?" The magic was still thick, but it had stopped building in intensity. It felt like the whole world had stopped to listen to Stonecrow's voice.

The other woman gave a cry. "Brian!"

Magic surged, hard and sudden.

I sneezed.

There was no drumming to cover my ass this time. There was a clattering of bones as Stonecrow whirled to stare at me, only halfway concealed by the corner of the mausoleum. The candlelight from the tapers lit up the side of her face, giving me a glimpse of a very beautiful woman. She had big lips. I'd always liked big lips.

Crimson striped her cheeks, nose, throat, breasts. Was that...blood?

She lifted the mallet for the drums in one hand like she was going to hurl it at me.

"Who's there?"

So much for sneaking up on her. I stood and put a hand on my holster. "Isobel Stonecrow, you are under arrest for necromancy."

Her clients didn't need to hear anything else. They turned tail and fled down the hill toward their red Lexus. The woman was wearing three-inch heels, so it was a slow fleeing. At another time, it would have been funny to watch her stagger through the mud.

Stonecrow flung the mallet at me. I ducked. It twirled harmlessly over my shoulder.

In two strides, I had crossed the space between us and seized her wrist. Her headdress held back straight brown hair. She wore a necklace of bones around her neck, interspersed with white and black beads. And holy hell, that really was all she was wearing above the waist. Her nipples were encircled by blood, too.

If Pops ever caught one of my cousins in public like that, she'd have been sitting tender for a week. Me? I didn't mind so much. But it's not good to stare at the suspects.

"Let go!" she cried, trying to yank free of my grip. She had obviously never fought a guy twice her body mass before. She didn't get anywhere with it.

"I'm Agent Cèsar Hawke with the Office of Preternatural Affairs, Magical Violations Department." I automatically reached for the cuffs on my belt only to realize that I didn't have them. I never went anywhere without my handcuffs. What had I done with them?

Right. They had taken a vacation on my headboard the night Erin died, so the cuffs were probably in an evidence locker right about now.

My eyes swept over the ritual scene. Her circle was small, and now that I had crossed her salt line, it wasn't resonating magic. The candles had melted into place on top of Brian Stewart's gravestone.

Add the drum and incense and animal bones to the mix, and I was certain I could prove she had been doing magic in front of mundane humans, if nothing else. Definitely an arrest-worthy offense.

Too bad I wasn't taking her back to the OPA offices.

"We're going to have a talk," I said. Maybe in one of the mausoleums.

She kicked at my knees with sandaled feet. I grunted and hauled her down the hill toward a slightly more hospitable-looking tomb.

"Let me go! This wasn't supposed to happen tonight! He told me I could do another job!"

What the hell was she talking about? And more importantly... "Are these cat bones?" I interrupted, shaking her wrist.

She gave her bracelets a surprised look, as if seeing them for the first time. "Raccoon."

Well, at least Cat was safe from her.

Eyes on the road watching for other OPA agents, I pushed her toward the tomb. She stopped dead when we came out from behind the trees.

"Where's your SUV?" Stonecrow asked, glaring at the parking lot.

Shit. She had obviously seen us before. We drove big black SUVs, much like the Union, though ours had lights and plates like the FBI's did. And the fact that I didn't have one now was, apparently, a big fucking giveaway.

I really should have borrowed Suzy's handcuffs.

"Traitor!" she hissed.

With surprising speed, Stonecrow wrenched

free of my grip. The bone bracelet snapped, leaving me holding a fistful of raccoon ribs and what looked like a car key dangling among them. I wasn't even sure how she'd escaped me. She must have been feigning weakness when I first grabbed her.

Stonecrow reached into her animal skins and pulled out a fistful of gray powder. My eyebrows lifted, and I couldn't help but grin a little bit. She looked like she was naked under her butt-flap. Did I want to know where she had been storing that dirt? Probably not.

"Stand down or I'll shoot," I said.

I made it two steps down the hill before she flung the powder into my eyes.

It was like having a beehive tossed in my face. I crashed to my knees with a roar, clawing ineffectually at my eyes. *Fuck*, that burned. Fire swept up my jaw, cheeks, forehead. Blisters bubbled under my hands. They popped. Gushed down into my collar.

There was no surge of magic and not a single sound, but by the time my running eyes cleared, Isobel Stonecrow was gone.

CHAPTER TEN

I STAGGERED INTO THE public library as soon as the librarian unlocked the door. She stepped back, giving me a wide berth and a shocked look.

"Oh my," she said, crossing herself as she scurried inside. I might not have been popular with the ladies, but I wasn't "turn pale and run away" ugly. That was a bad sign. Real bad.

Slamming into the lobby bathroom, I flipped on the light switch. Considering how old and musty the building had looked from outside, the place sure got painfully bright, like jabbing huge fucking knives into my eye sockets. And, unfortunately, it let me see what Stonecrow had done to my face.

My square features were covered in boils. The left side was bad, but the right side was worse. My eyelids were swollen, lip sagging with the weight of pustules.

Fuck. This was *not* one of my better weeks.

I splashed water on myself to get off the last of that nasty gray powder and tried to decide what, if anything, I could do about it. It was more uncomfortable than painful now. Little Tylenol and it probably wouldn't ache.

I poked one of the boils on my chin. It broke and made an audible *splat* against the porcelain sink. Underneath, the skin looked raw and red.

Pops's wise advice about popping zits echoed out of distant teenage memory.

You should pop every zit that you want to turn into a permanent scar, he'd said. And he had punctuated that with, *Dumbass*.

He hadn't intended that advice for magicked boils, but it probably applied.

Yeah, maybe I'll just leave them alone. For now.

On the bright side, Stonecrow had given me a great disguise. A disguise that made it feel like my entire face was peeling apart, with pus dripping down my neck. But I couldn't manage to feel grateful for it. I swore right then and there that I was going to see that woman behind bars—even if it meant turning myself over to the OPA, too.

I headed out of the bathroom, keeping my head down and trying to look like any other homeless bum making his way for the computer desks. I parked my ass in the first empty desk chair I came across. The old woman next to me didn't even look up when I sat down. But Gramps across the table cringed at the sight of me, grabbed his jacket, and left.

"Hey, ugly fuckers are people, too," I muttered at his back. The corner of my mouth cracked.

I pulled Stonecrow's case file out of my coat, opened a map site on the computer, and started correlating the coordinates of her previous sightings to the website. The locations of the last families she had scammed—the ones I'd read about earlier that night—got little flags first, smack dab on the big population centers in the state. If I'd been at work, that would have been enough for the computers to do a quick sweep and figure out the connection. But I wasn't at work. I'd have to do all the thinking for myself.

As I added the rest of the sightings aggregated from the OPA's network of security cameras, a pattern started to appear. I absently scratched my chin while I looked at them and felt something warm ooze down my jaw. *Okay, no scratching, either.*

I focused on the Stonecrow sightings. And when I pulled out her raccoon bone bracelet for another look at the car key I'd grabbed, I realized it wasn't a car key at all.

It was a key for an RV.

The old lady at the neighboring computer lumbered out of her chair and vanished. She left all of her crap on the desk, including an empty water bottle and a cell phone. It was scattered everywhere. Encroaching on my space. I didn't care if she was going to look for another book or going to take a piss. No one was respectful of public space anymore.

I picked up the phone and dialed Suzy.

"Why the fuck are you calling me?" she said when I identified myself. "Tell me you're out of town, Hawke."

"Nice to talk to you, too. Listen, I need you to pull files for me."

"What? Are you *working* right now?"

She tore me a new one for a minute, and except

for a quick look around to make sure Grandma Space Hogger wasn't on her way back, I kicked back and let Suzy's vitriol wash over me. It was soothing, in its own way. Familiar. The dulcet background sounds I was used to at the office.

"Feel better?" I asked when she wound down.

"Hmph. That's what you get for taking off without leaving a note, asshole." I heard the clatter of computer keys on the other end of the line. "Okay, what files am I pulling?"

"Any RVs that have checked in at more than five of these California RV parks in the last three months." I listed the locations off. Suzy typed furiously.

"Huh," she said. "One RV comes up. Registration for…Belle Stonecrow. You're still after the necromancer?"

"Actually, I think she's necrocognitive, like Peter was before he—you know. She's not raising zombies, that's for sure."

"Stonecrow is *my* case, Hawke."

"I'm helping you find her. You can think of it as me paying you back for use of your couch last night."

"Whatever." Suzy couldn't conceal how excited she sounded. It was a breakthrough. A good breakthrough. This was the shit that fueled us.

Isobel Stonecrow was living out of RV parks. It was so simple, and considering how much crap witches needed to lug around, practical as hell. Better than sleeping in the back of a car, too.

"Thanks," I said. "I'll find her."

I was about to hang up when Suzy said, "You

wouldn't leave if I told you to again, would you?"

"Not a chance."

I was in good shape. Not like the guys in the Union, but I kept up with my cardio. So I managed to reach the first two RV parks by noon with the help of a couple of city buses. No Stonecrow. I took a break around noon, stopping in a burger joint to escape the rain and splurge on dollar cheeseburgers. Bargain menus had saved my bacon between paychecks before.

The cheeseburgers would've been *so good* with bacon.

The third RV park took a longer, deeply unnerving bus ride to reach, and it was in the bad part of town. Know how they talk about "wrong side of the tracks?" Well, it looked like this park had been planted solidly in the middle of those tracks and then run over a few dozen times by trains hauling thousands of cattle, each of which took a giant dump on the park as it passed.

It was inside a crumbling brick wall. The smell of rain failed to overpower the sewage stench of a couple dozen RVs dumping their shit all over the place. Every so-called "recreational" vehicle looked like it had survived a nuclear blast.

If radioactive hillbillies ever vacationed in Los Angeles, this would have been the spot.

"You okay, dude?" the man at the window of the third RV park asked as I stopped to catch my breath. "Don't die on my sidewalk, man. I gotta clean this thing."

I knew I looked bad, but on-the-verge-of-death bad? And people said that no one cared in this town. "I'm fine." I took a few deep breaths and regretted it. Man, that smell was terrible. Hard to tell if it was coming from the park or the guy operating the gates. He looked like a radioactive hillbilly himself, mostly bald with more hairy moles than teeth. "I'm actually looking for a friend."

I went through the whole deal, miming Stonecrow's height against mine, tracing her more slender form and generous hips. The man's eyes lit up for a second, but then his face went neutral.

"Dunno," he said, scratching the mole on the left side of his neck. His fingernail was yellow and cracked. "My memory's terrible."

And me without money for a bribe.

"Thanks anyway," I said.

The man looked disappointed. "Any time, bro."

I made like I was walking down the street, away from the entrance.

As soon as I was out of sight of the office, I vaulted the brick wall and dropped down on the other side behind an RV.

The look that guy had given me when I described Stonecrow was the look of a man that had seen ungodly perfection in a woman. The kind of woman with hips that could knock down walls, and her breasts—*Lord, those breasts*. No wonder clients had been paying thousands of dollars for her time.

I slipped my hand into my pocket and clenched it around Stonecrow's bracelet. The raccoon bones dug into my palm. The pain was enough of a reminder of what I was doing there, what I needed to do, and why.

Last time I'd let my balls do the thinking, I'd ended up with an innocent woman dead in my bathtub. And this particular woman, this necrocognitive, was the only way I was going to get justice for Erin. That's all she was. A tool to clear my name and find the real villain.

A tool that was slinking around behind the RV three parking spots down.

The sight of her lurking just a few yards away jolted me to my core. I hadn't expected to be so quick to find her, especially when she was already on the run again. I'd hoped to catch her off-guard, cozy and unsuspecting in her mobile escape unit. Instead, she was crouched behind an old RV that was decorated with beaded curtains and electric teal paint.

There were no animal skins in sight this afternoon. Stonecrow wore cutoff shorts and a baggy pullover. The only reason I could identify her at that distance was that she had feathers woven into her hair, like a faint echo of the elaborate headdress she had been wearing early that morning.

For a second, I thought Stonecrow had been clued in to my presence and was trying to sneak away. But she wasn't looking at me. She was leaning around the corner of the RV to peer at something else.

I followed her gaze to see a black SUV parked on the other side of her vehicle. It had flashing lights set into the grille and dark-tinted windows.

A pair of men in black suits stepped out. They were big guys, so much broader than me that they made me look like a skinny-assed nerd. Their necks were thick as tree trunks. Every move looked deliberate, choreographed. Only one type of person moved like that: kopides. Super-powered demon hunters.

The Union had found Stonecrow.

Wild thoughts whirled through my skull. Had Suzy reported our findings to her superiors, even knowing that I was going to the same place? Maybe she'd thought that they could get to Stonecrow first. Take away my primary incentive for remaining in town. No way she'd deliberately attempted to fuck up my day.

Whether or not it was what she had planned, that was definitely the outcome.

Stonecrow jumped into the shadows behind the next SUV, which was rocking on its suspension, like there was a dance party inside. Or some other kind of party. Then she jumped behind the next. The same one that I was hiding behind.

That was when she saw me. Horror flashed in her eyes.

Yeah, she recognized the blisters.

"*You,*" she hissed.

I lifted her bracelet. "Got something for you."

She snatched it out of my hand then turned to bolt.

I grabbed her by the upper arm. Stonecrow twisted and just about melted out of my grip again. I was ready for her this time. Seizing both of her wrists, I shoved her back against the brick wall, giving her no room to pull off ninja maneuvers.

"Your bosses can't have me," Stonecrow spat. "I'd rather bury myself alive."

"I'm not taking you to anyone else. I don't want to hurt you."

Doubt flickered through her eyes. They were dark brown, the color of rain-moistened grave dirt. "You're not with them?"

"Yeah, right, glad we're on the same page. We gotta get out of here before they see us," I whispered. "Can you climb the fence?"

"I could if I had use of my hands." She wasn't fighting me anymore. I relaxed my grip on her.

Stonecrow kneed me between the legs.

It was like having a hot poker shoved into the middle of my intestines and then twisted. Nausea spread over my skin, from the tips of my hair to my fingernails, and I momentarily entertained the mental image of vomiting in her face.

My grunt of surprise was louder than I intended. By the time Stonecrow grabbed the brick wall and hefted her body halfway up, the Union suits were breaking past the line of RVs, searching for the source of the noise.

Eyes fell on me.

I realized that I recognized these guys. They weren't just any random, anonymous Union apes; they were Joey and Eduardo, Suzy's drinking buddies. Nice couple of young guys. Both of them had more muscles than brains and twice the strength of normal human men. Any doubts I'd had about Suzy tipping off her superiors were gone.

They ran at me as fast as they could sprint, which was, unfortunately, way too fast. Super strength comes with super speed. Not like the Flash or Superman, but a hell of a lot faster than me.

Eduardo grabbed for the back of the necrocognitive's sweater and missed. He caught her hair instead, jerking her to the ground, pulling out a fistful of her glossy black locks as he did it. I didn't think that was in the Union playbook.

"Hey!" I protested, just as Joey punched me in the gut. It was a little too close to where Stonecrow had hit. I crumpled. Even a big tough guy starts crying for Mama when the *juevos* take a double tap. Low blow from another dude, especially one who'd been buying me shots of tequila the other night. *Real* low blow.

"What do we do with this…thing?" Joey asked.

Eduardo shrugged. "Tie him up, toss him somewhere dark? Wait." He peered closely at my face then began to laugh. "Oh, that's too fucking good. Joe, check him out. Suzy was right."

Now they were both laughing. After a second, I worked up a halfhearted smile, trying to chuckle along. I probably would have laughed at them if they got dusted in the face, too. "Yeah, it's me. Suzy sent you this way to pick me up?"

"No, just Stonecrow," Eduardo said. "None of us thought you'd be dumb enough to show up too."

Guess I was that dumb. "You want to untie me now?"

Joey punched me in the stomach again. I fell to

my knees.

"Guess not," I gasped.

"So?" Joey asked.

After a moment of silent deliberation, Eduardo seemed to come to a decision. "We'll just take care of both of them. Lucky day, Joey, lucky day."

I tried to feel satisfied at the sight of Stonecrow's wrists zip tied and her petite form hauled toward the black SUVs, but even though it was her fault that I was in custody, I couldn't work up the satisfaction. This was *my* necrocognitive. Not the Union's. And I didn't like it when any woman got treated like a piece of meat, even if she'd worked hard at deserving it.

"Come on, guys," I said. "You're asking for about six different citations with this behavior."

"Shut up, Hawke," Joey said. He pushed my wrists together and zip tied them.

My heart climbed into my throat, thudding with panic, as Joey opened the back door of the SUV and I came face to face with the yawning maw of its interior.

Briefly, I pitied everyone we'd ever made disappear into one of these black cars.

Then I was inside and the door slammed behind me.

CHAPTER ELEVEN

NOTE TO SELF: BEING arrested by the Union sucks.

As it turned out, our guys were crazy fucking drivers. When Eduardo wasn't hitting the brakes so hard that my head nearly snapped off my neck, he seemed to be veering around to catch every pothole under his tires.

"Hope you're not too fond of the suspension," I called to the front. I got one sunglassed glare over Eduardo's shoulder.

Neither of them seemed interested in anything I had to say. Joey was talking into a cell phone too quietly for me to hear, and Eduardo was keeping up with his shitty driving.

It was guys like him that made my morning commute a joy.

"What are you doing talking back?" Stonecrow asked in a low whisper. "You want to make this worse?"

Worse? My face looked like ground fucking beef, I was under arrest by my own employer, and the necrocognitive I'd hoped would exonerate me was about to get tossed into a detention center far beyond my reach. And she thought a little snark was going to make it *worse*?

"You don't get to talk. You got me into this." My pissed-off face was much better than these punks could muster, but Stonecrow didn't seem fazed.

"You got yourself into…whatever this is." She was looking pale.

"Either way, we're both being taken to an OPA field office for questioning." I glared at her. "Have you been interrogated before? I've been on the other side of it, so I can give some pointers."

"I can handle myself."

"Sure, whatever." I rolled my shoulders to keep them from getting tense and raised my voice again. "We getting to the office soon? I've got to piss like a racehorse."

No one answered me.

Fuck all this bullshit. I wasn't letting Suzy's mix-up land me in prison.

We were going to get out of this.

"Don't suppose you got any of that dust left over?" I asked Stonecrow quietly. I didn't think boils were going to do much to slow down Eduardo and Joey, hardened kopides that they were, but enchanted dust could be useful for other reasons. I could try to change it, use its power.

"They patted me down, asshole. They took all the supplies I had." She pulled a face. "And copped a feel while they were at it."

They hadn't fondled me, but they'd taken all of my notebooks, too. And the gun that had been bouncing uselessly against my hip. And the

Stonecrow file. I'd thought I had nothing when I had to flee my apartment, but now I *really* had nothing. At least Stonecrow would still have her hideous teal RV if she escaped.

Stonecrow gave me a scrutinizing look. "If you're not with them, then why did you assault me during my job last night?"

"You mean the creepy death ritual."

"That's my *job*," she said.

"First of all, I wasn't assaulting you. I was taking you into custody. Big difference. Second of all, I've been looking for you to ask for help. I wanted you to use the creepy death ritual to talk to someone."

Stonecrow sniffed at me. "You've been near death recently."

Yeah, because *that* was hard to guess.

"I was just in a cemetery. Remember?"

"No, not that." Her eyes trailed over me, intense and focused. Under different circumstances, it would have been a nice look to get. "Who was killed?"

"That's what I was going to have you help me with before…" I jerked my chin at the dashboard of the car, indicating Eduardo and Joey.

That was when I realized that we weren't in the city anymore.

The freeway had turned into a highway outside the city at some point, and there wasn't any stop-and-go traffic left. The buildings had thinned out, and sandy hills decorated with brush surrounded the road.

"What's wrong now?" Stonecrow asked.

"We're not going to the office." I looked out the back window like that would change what I was seeing. It didn't. Los Angeles was a quickly vanishing memory behind us. The closest field office to the RV park was in the complete opposite direction. We were headed into the deep desert instead.

"You got *anything* in your bag of tricks?" I muttered as the SUV pulled off onto a dirt road away from traffic entirely. Not that dropping my voice meant anything at that point. We didn't have much time. "Something distracting? Flash powder? Poison ivy?"

"Why would I—what's going on?"

"I just need something magical!"

Grudgingly, Stonecrow squirmed onto her side, rolling her hip to offer her back pocket to me. No, not her pocket—it was empty, flat and smooth against her butt. "Underwear. Left side." She whispered so quietly I could barely hear her.

Whoa. Okay.

I tried not to touch her too much as I wiggled a plastic bag out from under the elastic band of her underwear. Black lace. *Damn.* She'd tucked the bag inside the folded-over hem, concealing a couple grams of a gray powder that looked a lot like what she had used to fuck up my face.

"I thought you were all out," I hissed.

She sat back. "I lied."

Joey glanced at me over his shoulder, still talking on the phone, and I palmed the baggie.

Rubbing my thumb on the plastic, I tried to guess what was inside. Definitely some salt.

Looked like a little grave dirt—I used it in many of my poultices, so I was pretty sure about that one. Maybe some nettle, too. It was only lightly enchanted.

It would have to be enough.

"Where are you taking us?" I asked, louder than before, making sure I'd be heard over the engine.

"I'm going to do it now," Eduardo said. He wasn't speaking to me.

"Not until we're out of town," Joey said. "Follow the plan."

The plan. Between our eastward travels and their mutterings, I was *not* feeling good about this "plan."

I knew the Union had more outposts than the OPA did. We were mostly a bureaucratic affair—the brain to the Union's body. They had fingers in everything, everywhere. For all I knew, they had a hidden base out this way and we were being sent there. But it wasn't a base I knew.

If they were taking me somewhere that I didn't have high enough clearance to see, then chances were good I wasn't meant to come back.

Eduardo and Joey were focused away from us again. I opened the bag and carefully poured the gray dust in a tiny circle on the seat between Stonecrow and me. Her eyes widened, anger flashing over her face. She thought I was wasting it. In fact, I was casting the smallest fucking circle of power ever. Wondered if I might break a world record.

I poked the dust toward the north, south, east,

west. The highway was straight as far as I could see—had to finish casting the spell before we hit a turn and messed up the orientation.

Pouring the last of the dust in the center, I snapped my fingers and closed the circle.

The magical juice inside was small enough that I didn't even sneeze. It barely even tickled.

"With earth and stone, I call strength," I whispered under my breath, pushing all of my meager energy into the circle, building its force with my own spirit. "With salt and…uh…"

"Nettle," Stonecrow said.

My guess had been right. Nice. "With salt and nettle, I call strength. With the desert around us, I call strength." Yeah, I know, it was stupid, but I'm not a poet. I don't get fancy with my words.

But it was enough. I could see faint, coppery sparks of magic igniting within the powder.

Strength spells were one of my only specialties. Like the poultices I kept by the bed to juice up my muscles. Even a big guy can use a small edge when all of his foes are supernatural. I'd been making them daily, like protein shakes, for years. And that was probably the only reason my tiny, miserable circle of power was actually working, infusing the dust in the center with energy.

What else could I use against Eduardo and Joey? I needed *something*.

My mind touched on Domingo. The kind of shit he used to pull in high school while gambling. Luck spells.

"With the wind and sun, grant me luck," I added, and I blew gently on the dust, focusing every ounce of my concentration on my brother.

Gold sparks. Copper sparks.

Pretty pathetic magic right there.

And I was out of time. There was a bend in the road coming up, but Eduardo was signaling and slowing the car, suggesting that our trip was over.

There were no buildings outside, no secret Union base. Just empty desert between a few isolated hills.

Shit.

I broke the tiny circle and pinched the gram of dust that I had infused with strength and luck. It burned against my fingers, but there were no blisters. I'd repurposed the magic for a more positive use, and I could only pray that my shitty spell would work. I still couldn't help but flinch as I sprinkled it on my tongue.

I sneezed.

The SUV stopped with a jerk. Joey jumped out, flung my door open.

"Get out," he said, aiming a gun at my head.

"This isn't Union procedure." I was delaying, scooping the rest of the powder into my hand. The properties of the stuff I'd used to make the circle hadn't changed, and it still burned. I could feel my palm rippling with new boils. I clenched my fist around it.

I eased away from Stonecrow as casually as I could. Just my hands in a zip tie and my life in tatters, nothing to see here. She struggled when Eduardo grabbed her, but they were as well trained as I was and much better prepared. I just had to hope Stonecrow's distraction could give me a few seconds.

Outside it was even brighter and hotter than it had been in the city. I was sweating when they pulled me out. I stumbled and fell onto my knees.

Joey pulled me to my feet again and dragged me when I didn't get up fast enough. He was six inches shorter than me and twice as strong. But I could feel the powder on my tongue tingling, and the strength in my muscles was growing quickly with a familiar buzz.

My shitty spell had worked. Better still, it had worked *well*. My limbs felt limber and strong. My head was light. Everything fell into hyper-focus—probably the luck part of the spell.

It felt great. Good enough that I didn't even panic when I noticed the manmade ditch that had been carved into the side of the road just off the shoulder.

The kopis kicked me behind the knees, making me fall on the edge. And then I felt a gun in the back of my head.

It was a by-the-book roadside execution. They would blow our brains out, leave us out of sight of the few people who even come out this way for off-roading, let the coyotes pick our bleached bones.

Definitely not Union procedure.

But I didn't know that for a fact—maybe this was what the Union did when they black bagged people. Maybe everyone I'd ever arrested had ended up in a ditch in the desert.

Or maybe these fuckers were working for the asshole who had framed me for murder.

Either way, I wasn't going down. My heart was

pounding and I was smiling.

"Say a prayer," Joey said, pushing the barrel hard into the back of my neck.

This should have been so much scarier than it was.

Lifting my bound, burning hands into a prayer position, I began to speak. "Hail Mary, full of grace, hallowed be thy name. Thy kingdom come, something, something, Heaven...and fuck you, asshole. Amen."

I twisted and flung the remaining dust into Joey's face.

A gunshot exploded next to my left ear.

So much for hearing.

His mouth opened in a roar that I couldn't hear. He fell, dropping the gun, clawing at his face. His skin was rippling and twisting. Watching the boils rise was almost worse than feeling it happen.

Almost.

Eduardo dropped his grip on Stonecrow's arm and aimed his gun at me. She was gone in an instant, rocketing toward the SUV with its open doors.

Good. One less thing to worry about.

I lunged to my feet and drove my shoulder into Eduardo's gut, knocking the breath out of him. I managed to throw his ass to the ground. Jerked the gun out of his hand. My fingers were too swollen from the dust to grip it properly. I fumbled, dropping it.

Joey and his Elephant Man features were coming after me again. I kicked sand into his face—into those open, oozing wounds. He screamed.

Eduardo was getting up again. I swung my tethered fists at him and struck. He grunted, tried to punch me, and missed. He barely managed to claw at my face as he fell. My own boils erupted, pouring pus down my jaw.

Both of them regained their footing and jumped on me at the same time. We scuffled, and I didn't know who was yelling and which guy was elbowing me. Feet and fists slammed into me. I curled up, protected my head. Managed to kick Joey to the ground, and he stayed down. But Eduardo didn't.

When I glanced through my arms, he was drawing a gun from his jacket. He aimed it at my forehead.

All the supernatural ways I could've gone out in this world, and a bullet between the eyes was going to finish me.

How boring.

The gunshot rang in my ears.

But I wasn't in pain.

I wasn't dead, either.

It took me a second to sit up and figure what had happened. Eduardo was on the ground next to me, also still alive, but out cold. Stonecrow was holding a bloody rock in one fist, looking shocked that she had actually managed to bash it into his skull hard enough to do damage.

I'd thought Stonecrow had run for it and left me behind, but she had saved me.

I managed a grin for her.

Joey was getting up behind her, preparing to sneak up while she was distracted. I got to my feet and kicked him a few times in the gut, knocking him back down to the dirt. And then I kicked him in the face. Pustules exploded all over the desert.

"Thanks," Stonecrow said, pushing a lock of hair out of her face with the back of her wrist. She left a smear of blood and dust on her temple.

I kicked Joey again, just because.

"You're welcome," I said.

There were more zip ties in the SUV, so once Stonecrow and I had cut free of our restraints, I used them on Eduardo and Joey. They were both awake when I finished. Eduardo seemed like he was having a hard time staying awake, head lolling—he might have had a concussion, but I didn't really care. Joey was much more conscious and much uglier.

I crouched in front of them. The sun was at their back because I was nice like that. Evening was coming fast. They might not even get sunburned before it got dark again.

"So how was this supposed to end?" I asked. "Was it secret Union procedure, or something personal?"

Instead of answering, Joey said, "Are you fucking stupid?"

Well, yeah, that was a possibility. But I wasn't the one tied up in a ditch. I couldn't be *that* stupid.

Eduardo worked his mouth around, gathering saliva on his tongue, then spat on the ground at my feet.

Nice.

Stonecrow jiggled my shoulder before I could ask more questions. I brushed her off, but she did it again. "What?"

"Shouldn't we be leaving?" She was looking at the abandoned SUV.

She had a point. All of the OPA's cars had GPS trackers in them. Just because we were alone for the moment didn't mean that we'd be alone for long. "Works for me." I patted my pockets and made sure my notebooks were where I'd put them. I'd grabbed all of my stuff out of the SUV while looking for the zip ties, and the desert would've been a bad place to accidentally drop them. "Let's get out of here."

"You can't just leave us here!" Joey cried as we walked toward the car.

I didn't tell him we could. Actions spoke louder than words.

Anyway, it wouldn't be long before the Union picked them up.

Unfortunately.

I yanked the cable to the GPS tracker under the car before taking off again.

Once we were back on the highway, I pulled the phone out of my pocket and tossed it into Stonecrow's lap. "I'll read you a number, and I want you text this location to the number."

"What location? I've got no clue where the hell we are."

I parked the car by the side of the road. "Here, I'll do it."

She didn't let me pull the phone from her hands.

I rubbed my forehead then winced. I was still covered in blisters. The sun had only made it worse. "You can pull our coordinates up on the app on the phone. Give it to me."

She scowled but obeyed. I grabbed our coordinates from the phone and texted them to Suzy with a short message: "Eduardo and Joey tried to kill me. Get to them first and find out why." I waited for the message to go through, then handed the phone back to Stonecrow.

"We should get rid of that," I said. "It has a GPS tracker, too. I'll let you decide how to trash it."

Stonecrow stepped out of the car and ducked. When she got back in and closed the door with a solid *thump*, I raised an eyebrow in her direction. She said, "Under the tire." The corner of her mouth twitched as she surveyed me. "You look like shit."

I angled the rearview mirror. *Yep, still hamburger-faced*. "Wonder why that is."

"I can fix it," Stonecrow said. "I just need some herbs."

Her tone wasn't exactly friendly, but she didn't sound pissed at me now. It was a start. And if she could heal my face? Better and better.

The phone crunched when I pulled away.

We rode in silence, Stonecrow only moving to turn on the air conditioning. The quiet lasted on the road back to town for about five minutes or so when she said, "So…Cèsar, right? You didn't kill the agents back there. Because you work with them?"

"I don't know if they deserve killing. And that's not something I do, anyway. But yeah, I kinda work with them—or at least I used to. I'm currently taking what you might call an unscheduled vacation from the Office of Preternatural Affairs."

"Why?"

No nice way to say it. "Because I've been accused of murder."

Stonecrow leaned toward her window a few inches.

"Oh."

"I didn't do it," I said. "That's why I need your help. I need you to talk to the victim and find out who did kill her. It's the only way I can clear my name."

She let out a shaky breath. "Okay. Tell me what happened. Tell me about *her*." I gave her the short version of Erin's story. It wasn't much shorter than the long version. When I finished, Stonecrow was frowning more than ever. "So you…you *didn't* kill this waitress?"

Could she have tried to sound a little less skeptical?

"No. I didn't."

"And you want me to talk to her."

It was like we were talking in circles. "If you can do what you say you can."

"I can," Stonecrow said, tapping her finger thoughtfully against her chin. "I just need to get close to her remains, preferably within touching distance. You think you can pull that off with people gunning for your head? Do you think you even *want* to? It'd be much safer to run."

"I've gotten this far. I can't stop now."

She sighed. "Okay. Let's go talk with Erin."

CHAPTER TWELVE

WE MADE A STOP at an herb shop then grabbed dinner at a fast food joint as the sun sank to the horizon. Dinner and magical supplies were paid for by Joey, who turned out to have a fat wallet. I left the credit cards and his fake FBI identification in the glove box. The cash was ours.

I didn't risk going inside the McDonald's to order. We went through the drive-through and ate behind the security of tinted windows in the parking lot. Stonecrow looked extremely disinterested in my burgers, but she seemed okay with her chicken wrap, and she guzzled her soda in about five seconds flat.

"So what's your story?" I asked when I was halfway through my meal, gesturing at her. "What does the OPA want you for?"

"They don't tell you that in your files?"

"Your file says that you've had three families complain that you're a scam artist. But every story's got two sides, right?"

"Three complaints." She snorted. "The dead don't lie, Cèsar. That's why people complain. They don't like what the dead have to say to them. I haven't done anything wrong."

Stonecrow wiped her fingers with one of the paper napkins. She looked around for a place to throw it out and caught sight of her dirty face in the mirror. We were both all dusty from the brawl in the desert. She used other napkins to wipe off her face.

"Necrocognition is a rare talent."

"Is it?" Stonecrow asked. I couldn't tell if she was being sarcastic or not.

"Where'd you learn to do it? Are you part of some kind of…I dunno, a tribe or something?" I asked. Her getup at Shady Groves had looked like the fifties Hollywood idea of a Native American wisewoman, but I had a hard time believing that that anyone who wore feathered headdresses and animal skins to a cemetery could be legit.

Yet she sat up straighter, tossed her hair. Her whole demeanor shifted. It was like she pulled on a disguise as I watched. "Yes, my tribe taught me. I am a native princess. I was trained by the best shamans in all of the nations," she said, voice resonant with that accent she'd had before. "I was going to stay on our reservation, but the spirits called me to the world beyond. It is my destiny to speak the truths of the dead even when people aren't prepared to hear it."

"That so?"

"You saw how those Union men behaved when they arrested me—what they were prepared to do to silence the voices of the dead." She sounded both imperious and annoyed. I guess my incredulity was showing.

"I have a hard time believing the Union would try to kill you if you can do what you claim. You're too valuable. Hell, I bet the OPA would love to hire you."

"You can deny it all you want, but it's obvious that those men didn't intend for you and I to come back from the desert."

That much, I couldn't deny. I just didn't know why.

She tossed her trash in the backseat and grabbed the plastic bag from between her feet. I'd let her do all the buying in the herb shop and kept my aching face inside the SUV, so I had no idea what she'd gotten.

"So how does your necrocognition work? Is it an evocation thing?"

She glanced at me before opening a baggie and pouring something green and grainy into her empty soda cup. "What? What's evocation?"

For the first time since we'd started chatting, I believed the disbelief in her voice. It was more genuine than her bullshit "princess of the tribes" speech. "So you're not summoning demons in order to talk to the dead. Doing blood rituals and shit. Human sacrifice."

"I do use blood," she said. I grimaced, and she hastily added, "I get it from the butcher's. Pig, cow, chicken."

The thought of slaughtering animals for a spell didn't bother me—I'd knocked off a few mice and rats in my time training with the OPA—but witches that were willing to kill for power often didn't stop at animals. I watched Stonecrow warily as she mixed ingredients. After she'd tossed a few things into her cup, she replaced the plastic lid and shook it.

"I was impressed with your spell in the SUV," she said, softer than before. "That was great."

Great? Well, if that was the word she wanted to use for it, I wasn't going to stop her. "What can I say? Panic is inspirational. I don't even do ritual circles most of the time. I'm more of a potions and poultices kind of guy. My coworker, Suzy, she's all about the circles of power and energy manipulation. Bet she could have cooked up something even better." I laughed. "Bet she could have cursed both of them without even getting out of the car."

She lifted an eyebrow. "Well, you did well enough for both of us to survive."

Yeah, we'd survived. Couldn't ask for much more than that.

She took the lid off her cup again and scooped out a pulpy mess that smelled like a hamster cage. Stonecrow reached across the center console toward me.

I jerked back. "What's that?"

She grabbed the wrist of my blistered hand.

"Relief," Stonecrow said, smearing the mix on my skin.

The hot ache of the wound immediately subsided and was replaced by a damp coolness. Shivers rolled down my skin as the blisters dried, shriveled, and sloughed away to reveal fresh skin underneath.

It felt so good that I didn't stop her when she dabbed it on the rest of the blisters, too. The stench was overpowering, but not magical. I didn't even sneeze.

She handed me a fistful of napkins. "There you go."

I wiped my face clean and checked the mirror. I looked like Cèsar again. A Cèsar that desperately needed to shave, but Cèsar nonetheless.

Stonecrow was smiling a little, giving me a weird look.

"What's wrong?" I asked, tilting my jaw to see if I was turning purple or something.

"Nothing," she said. "It's just—I didn't get a good look at you in the cemetery before defending myself, so now I'm…looking at you." The smile seemed fixed to her lips.

Fuck if I knew why. Women.

"Thanks for the…" I drew a circle in the air around my face with a finger, indicating all the freshly healed skin. "Even if you caused the damage to it in the first place."

Her eyes had gone a little glassy as she gazed at me. She blinked and refocused. "Oh. Self-defense. I thought you were going to kill me." It wasn't exactly an apology. Guess I didn't need one. Stonecrow grabbed a clean napkin. "You missed a spot." She wiped along my jaw. I didn't think I'd missed anything, but I appreciated not smelling like hamster cage, so I let her clean down my neck and collar.

Once she was done with the pawing, I finished my last burger. The beef didn't taste quite as good now that she'd mentioned using animal blood in her rituals. "Let's get one thing straight, Stonecrow. If you're into human sacrifice for your magic, get out of the car right now. I don't work with murderers."

"Isobel," she said. "Not Stonecrow. Isobel's fine."

I liked the sound of that, but I didn't feel like being on first name terms with a murderess. "You haven't killed anyone for a magic spell," I pressed.

"Never," Isobel said.

Good enough. We could always talk about the animal cruelty later.

"Then let's have a talk with Erin," I said, turning the SUV on.

The night grew dark and sultry. It was nice enough out that I would have liked to roll down the windows and let the damp evening breeze into the car, but I was hesitant to give up what little privacy the tinted windows gave us. Not to mention the bulletproof glass. I could still feel the barrel of a gun jammed into the back of my skull. Now that the giddiness from my shitty luck/strength spell was wearing down, I could feel it *real* well.

I'd been one finger squeeze away from my brains splattered on the desert. That was enough to make a guy turn paranoid.

We parked outside Suzy's townhouse.

Isobel glanced out the window. "What's here?"

"My coworker. Suzy. She's gonna be able to help us."

"Suzy," she mused. "Bet she has blond pigtails."

More like pure animal rage and filthy jokes trapped inside a woman's body. Whatever. "Stay here," I said, and got out. When I rounded the car, Isobel was slamming her door, hiking her shorts up her ample hips. "Uh, didn't I say 'stay here?'"

"You said it," Isobel said, giving me a disarmingly dazzling smile.

Right.

She didn't follow me when I headed toward Suzy's blue door. She remained leaning against the SUV. I kept an eye on her as I headed up the walk.

I was on Suzy's front step, about to knock, when the door flew open. There must have been magical alarms that I hadn't sensed.

The instant of total relief on Suzy's face was immediately overwhelmed by anger. "Cèsar, you are one stupid motherfucker," she said, but she was grabbing me by the jacket, running her hands over my chest and arms, like she couldn't believe I was still alive. "What are you doing here? Are you okay? Did they hurt you?"

Considering that I hadn't gotten a bullet in the head? Yeah, I was feeling pretty thoroughly okay. "Did you get to Eduardo and Joey first? Did you question them?"

"Of course I didn't," she whispered. "The Union must have been ten seconds behind you. They recovered them first."

"So you don't know if executing people is Union procedure or if they'd been hired to kill us?"

"Executing people?" Suzy's eyes went wide

and round. Her fists clutched my lapels. "For fuck's sake, Cèsar, what the *fuck*? Who would have hired Eduardo and Joey as assassins anyway? They're dumbasses!" She shook her head. "No. They're good. They wouldn't—it couldn't have been bribes or something. They wouldn't do that."

Either Suzy didn't know her friends as well as I now did or it really was Union procedure to shoot people in the head the second they became nuisances. I wasn't sure which was worse.

She pressed her face to my chest, wrapped her arms around me for a tight squeeze, and then pulled back to punch me in the stomach. Damn, Suzy was a violent hugger. "*Fuck*, Cèsar. My texts are *monitored*. You stole a fucking Union SUV. You—" She cut off. She had finally noticed that I wasn't alone. "Who's that?"

Isobel was coming up the sidewalk. I opened my mouth to respond.

"You brought the necrocognitive to my *house*?" Suzy interrupted. "What the flying fuck is *wrong* with you, Cèsar?"

Leaning my shoulder against her doorway to block her view, I shrugged. "Bet if you asked Pops, he'd tell you he dropped me a few times as a kid. Look, Suzy, like I was saying, we need your help."

"*We*?"

Did she need to shout everything at me? "We need to find Erin Karwell's remains so we can talk to her and clear my name."

"*We*?"

Okay, she'd already said that.

Isobel touched my back. "Hey," she said. "Is

everything okay? You guys are...loud."

Suzy's expression shuttered. She looked between me and Isobel and the SUV with a weird look, brow furrowed, lips frowning. "I told you to get on a bus, Cèsar. I told you to run. I'm not going to help you serve your balls to the Union on a platter. We're done with this bullshit."

And then she slammed the door in my face.

"That was helpful," Isobel said brightly.

No fucking kidding.

CHAPTER THIRTEEN

WE GOT STUCK IN traffic after leaving Suzy's. I didn't know where we were going, so it didn't really matter. I just drove without stopping, creeping down the 5 Freeway slowly enough that I might as well have walked it.

The Union was probably tracking us now. We'd have to ditch the car soon—find another one. Where and how, I didn't know. I was exhausted and annoyed and my ability to plan had been left behind in the desert. I'd expected Suzy to have the answers—and access to Erin's body. Without either of those, I had no idea what to do next.

"Do you know where the OPA takes victims for autopsy?" Isobel asked.

Guess my aimlessness was obvious. "No," I admitted. "I never deal with murder. I specialize in picking up witches who've been getting into trouble, but generally not the homicidal type."

"More like the 'talking to the dead' type?" she asked with a teasing smile.

"If you're asking if you're one of my cases, yes. You are." I huffed out a breath. "Were." But she had the gears in my skull turning. Where *did* we take the dead? I'd never seen body bags hauled into my office building, but I had seen ambulances around. They probably went somewhere on the OPA campus.

The idea of breaking into one of our buildings was laughably bad. We had hundreds of magical and physical alarms—I'd have gotten arrested before I made it past the Starbucks between the Magical Violations and Infernal Relations buildings.

But maybe if someone could bring Erin's body out...

"How much body do you need?" I asked. "The whole thing, or would an arm or a finger work?"

Isobel pulled a face. "I don't know. I suppose I could do it with any part of the body."

Any part?

I cast my mind back to the blood in my bathroom. It might not have been cleaned up yet. And Erin had to have left some tissue behind, too.

We were almost past the exit closest to my apartment. I changed lanes without signaling, slicing through the narrow space between cars. Horns blared at me.

Isobel grabbed the leather arm of her chair. "What are you doing?"

"Getting you a piece of the victim."

We parked a few blocks away from my apartment building and walked the rest of the way there. I noticed that Isobel was carrying the bag from the herb shop with her, but didn't ask what else she had bought. She'd already admitted to using animal blood. I probably didn't want to know what she had in there.

It was a nice night for walking, even if I was out with a necrocognitive. The moon was hazy yellow, and the air was quiet and still. No signs of cops or Union anywhere. Didn't get any better than that.

Isobel eyeballed my building as we headed around back. "What is this place?"

"What, got a problem with it?"

Guess my defensiveness had given me away. She gave me a skeptical look. "You live *here*?"

I took another look at my apartment. It was indistinguishable from any of a million other apartment buildings in Los Angeles. The architecture was…well, it wasn't going to win any awards, but it wasn't like I spent much time looking at the big taupe box from the outside. It had a secure lobby and a couple trees. Whatever. I spent most of my time at the office anyway.

"You live in a teal RV with beaded curtains," I pointed out.

"Teal is a magical conductor. The curtains…" The corner of her mouth quirked. "Well, there's no excuse for that."

At least she was willing to admit it.

Grabbing the fire escape's ladder, I pulled it down and stepped aside.

"Ladies first," I said.

Isobel stared up at it. "I don't like heights."

"It's the only way up." I extended my hands toward her. "I won't let you fall."

She hesitated then climbed onto the first rung. I dutifully stood behind her, prepared to catch her in the unlikely event of the fire escape suddenly melting and throwing her to the ground. As soon as she reached the second floor, I followed her. And we did that all the way up to my floor.

When we got up to my apartment's window, Isobel glanced over the railing at the ground and turned pale. She grabbed my sleeve.

"I've got you," I said, steadying her.

She sighed and leaned against my chest, all warm and soft. Probably trying not to fall over. "You do have me, don't you?"

And with that weird question, she pushed in the screen for my window and slipped inside.

I climbed in after her.

My apartment hadn't changed since the last time I was there. I was relieved to see everything intact. The landlord was kind of a dick; I wouldn't have been surprised if he'd tossed all my belongings to the curb as soon as I went missing. But a cursory search proved that nothing new had gone missing since my last visit. The rent was paid through to the end of the month—maybe I could actually keep my home if I managed to clear my name before April rolled around.

Not that it felt like home anymore. I stood awkwardly in the bedroom as Isobel picked through my closet, staring at the bed that I'd woken up in on my last morning as an innocent man.

I'd been with Erin there. She'd died in this place. Shot and strangled.

I wasn't sure I could feel at home anywhere

ever again.

"What do you need out of my closet?" I asked.

"Oh, just looking around," she said airily, with a hint of that "shaman princess" tone. Yeah, right. She was snooping.

I pushed the door shut. "Look around somewhere else."

She lifted her hands in a gesture of surrender. "All right, all right."

"Need lights so that you can search for Erin's tissue?" I opened my bedside table in search of a flashlight.

She wandered out of the bedroom. "No, thanks. I don't need to see to find what I'm looking for."

I grabbed the flashlight anyway and turned it on. There was still blood on the hallway carpet. Isobel flinched at the sight of it. A little skittish for someone who had slapped animal blood on her bare breasts for a ritual in a cemetery.

"Getting any vibes?" I asked.

She shook her head slowly. "Where did Erin die?"

I led her to the bathroom. "The tub."

It was hard to stand there, staring at the empty bathtub, knowing what had been inside of it. But I had the necrocognitive. We were on the scene of the crime. If this were what I had to do to find Erin's killer—well, I'd do a hell of a lot worse to bring justice to her.

Isobel stopped beside me in the doorway. She swallowed hard.

"Do it," I urged. "Raise her."

Isobel kneeled on a clear patch of floor by the

tub, clutching her bag from the herb shop. Her face was ashen in the darkness. "So much blood," she whispered, trailing her hand over the edge of the tub. "How did she die?"

The memory of the bruised handprints on Erin's throat came to mind. "You tell me."

She clenched her jaw. Reached into the bag and sprinkled herbs across the floor. Thank God that was some kind of plant matter and nothing animal in origin. "Erin Karwell," Isobel said, one hand on the herbs, the other hand stretched over a tacky puddle of dried blood. She cleared her throat. When she spoke, she only had a trace of that dramatic, fake Indian accent. "I summon—I summon the spirits to…" She looked at me and trailed off.

"Well?" I demanded.

She put both hands on the tub and squeezed her eyes shut. "Erin Karwell," she whispered.

Isobel was silent for several long seconds. It was nothing like the cemetery. She wasn't even pretending to put on a show. She just…sat there. Doing nothing.

And after a minute, her eyes popped open again. "I don't have the right supplies." It sounded like she had to fight with herself to make the words come out, like she was confessing to something awful.

"What do you need?" There was a hard edge to my voice. Harder than I meant. "Do you need candles and salt? Do you need raccoon bones? Do you need to take off your shirt?"

"Cèsar…"

"Well?"

"I need a body."

"You've got her blood, you've got the herbs," I said. "Talk to the damn victim, Isobel!"

It exploded out of her. "I *can't*!"

The force of her frustration punched through me. I stepped back, gripping the doorframe.

So there was the truth. Isobel Stonecrow wasn't really a necrocog. She was a liar, a scammer. Exactly what the OPA had thought she was.

"The drums," I said. "The bones. The blood. Fake."

"Yes, all of that was fake," Isobel said, scattering the herbs across the bathroom floor as she stood. "And the herbs don't do anything, either, I was just—I always try to put on a show. But—"

I'd heard enough. I shoved away from the door.

"I can still help you, Cèsar! I just don't—"

"Forget about it," I said. The anger burned out of me, dwindling down into a hard iron core of defeat.

Isobel couldn't raise Erin. She couldn't give me the truth. I couldn't get vengeance—couldn't clear my name, get my job back, get my *life* back.

I didn't bother with the window. I ripped open the front door of the apartment, tore down the yellow police tape, and stalked away from the home I might never see again.

Isobel followed me to the top of the stairs and gazed at me with wounded eyes.

"Let me help you," she said. "We can still figure something out."

What the hell could a scammer do for me? For *Erin*? I froze on the landing and glared at her. "If you're smart, you'll get out of town, Stonecrow. And you won't come back."

Maybe that was what I should have done in the first place.

CHAPTER FOURTEEN

THE HOUSE I WAS standing in front of was by far the nicest I'd been to since this whole thing started, so long as you liked suburban sprawl—which I did. It was quiet on this street. The kind of place where everyone was in bed by nine and trouble didn't roam the sidewalks looking for things to tag with spray-paint. Trees were swaying with the breeze, a dog barked in the distance.

The guy who met me at the front door of the house on the corner looked like he belonged. Sweat suit, nice sneakers, crew-cut hair. His tattoos were hidden by sleeves. "I was wondering how long it would take for you to make your way here."

I sighed. "I didn't want to bring this to your door, but I just…I'm out of options, man."

Domingo pushed open the security screen and held his arms open. I stepped into his embrace, squeezed him tight. I'm not so much of a man that I can't hug my brother hard when I'm having a shitty week. Domingo hugged back just as fiercely.

"You look like shit on a stick. Do I want to know why?"

"I fought off two assassins in the desert. Kicked their asses. Pulled out all the ninja moves." I mimicked a few karate chops, and Domingo laughed.

"Sure you did. Couch in the den is yours as long as you want it."

I didn't want Domingo's couch at all. It was stiff and old, and Domingo's wife wouldn't be happy to see me on it.

What I really wanted was his ritual space.

Domingo and I had gotten into a lot of bad shit together as teenagers, but we'd gotten into a lot of good things, too. Like magic. Abuelita had been the one to identify that we had the old magic in the first place, taught us how to tap into it, but we'd worked together to find the limits of our abilities. Domingo still had an altar in his basement—everything a guy needed to whip up a batch of strength and energy potions.

The house was mostly dark when he let me in. It was well after midnight, but that shouldn't have mattered in my brother's house. He was a night owl.

I leaned around the end of his stairs to check the second floor. All the doors were open and the rooms were dark.

"Sofia already in bed?" I asked.

"She isn't here." A sigh. "We're taking a little time apart. And before you say it—"

"I wasn't going to say anything."

"—she's in love with someone else."

She wasn't my wife, but the announcement still felt like a punch to the face. I sucked in a hard breath. "You know who?"

"I don't, and I don't want to think about it." He scrubbed his hands through his hair. He'd always been the spitting image of our dad, except without the mustache. Now, with heartache etched on his face, he was practically Dad's twin. "Either she'll break it off with him or me, and I'll deal with either when it happens. You've got bigger problems. Sit down, I'll get you a beer."

"Shouldn't I clean up first?" I gestured at my dusty jacket and jeans.

"I'm not the one in the house who cares about the upholstery, dude."

There wasn't *anyone* in the house who cared about upholstery anymore. And his home felt a hell of a lot emptier for it.

I was the one on the run from murder charges, but I'd take my week over Domingo's. He was nuts for Sofia—she was his moon and stars and all that romantic crap. She was the reason he'd stopped knocking over 7-Elevens for petty cash and gotten a real job. She was the reason Domingo had a nice life in the first place.

I took the couch in the living room. It was a lot softer than the den couch.

"Anyone come looking for me?" I asked, eyeing Sofia's footstool and trying to decide if I wanted to risk putting my dirty shoes on it.

"You busted out of jail. What do you think?" Domingo called over his shoulder as he went for the kitchen. "Agent Takeuchi hit up Pops first, so I got the courtesy of a warning phone call before she appeared at my doorstep."

I whistled. "Suzy? Really?" I knew I'd probably been given a file like Isobel's and assigned to an agent, but I never would have thought that the OPA would assign me to my desk mate. Weird that it was the OPA visiting my family instead of the LAPD, though. "Did Pops have fun with her?"

"He says she's a gorgeous woman and you should let her catch you."

Of course he did. "Tell me he didn't hit on her."

"What do you think? Seventy-two years old and the man's still got it."

"He *thinks* he's got it, anyway," I muttered.

Domingo emerged from the kitchen and with two bottles of beer. I took mine gratefully and drank deep. The cold felt amazing going down my throat. And in my hand. I placed the bottle to my forehead and winced when it hit a bruise.

"Tell me what happened," Domingo said.

"What *hasn't* happened? I don't even know where to start."

"The beginning works."

The beginning. Right. "I had drinks. A lot of drinks. My coworkers and I were celebrating, and I tried to chat up a waitress—"

"Erin Karwell."

He knew her name. I grimaced. "Has it been on the news?"

"Oh yeah." He pushed a piece of paper across the coffee table to me. It was a printout from a news website. There was a picture of Erin on the top—gorgeous, innocent, living Erin, with her hair wild and a huge smile. The words in the headline, "Waitress Murdered," made me feel like I was falling down a deep, dark hole.

I skimmed the article. My name wasn't mentioned. One of the few advantages of being a spook, I guess.

"How'd you know that I was connected?" I asked, folding up the article, sticking it in my pocket. I wanted to keep Erin's face with me. A reminder of why I was doing what I was doing.

"The FBI agent," Domingo said. "She told us." He sank into the chair across from me, took a swig of beer. "She was acting real weird. I've never seen anyone that pissed in my life."

That didn't sound weird—that sounded like Suzy. I leaned back against the couch cushions, shut my eyes, rolled the sweating bottle over my face. "Don't look at me like that."

"You can't even see me right now."

"I don't have to see you." I opened my eyes. Domingo had schooled his face into something so innocent, it looped around about five times and landed right back on guilty. "I know what you're thinking. I always know what you're thinking. And Suzy didn't frame me for the murder."

"Someone did."

Lord, it was nice not having to be the first one to say it. A weight lifted from my lungs. I breathed for the first time in days. "Yeah. Someone did. But it wasn't Suzy."

"How can you be sure?"

If Suzy had framed me for the murder, then why would she have let me sleep on her couch? She had been nothing but a good friend. A better friend than I deserved. But I said, "She doesn't have a motive. Why kill a waitress?"

"You said you were hitting on this Erin girl, right?" Domingo asked. "Women get crazy when they're jealous."

Jealousy would have implied there was something between Suzy and me other than a cluttered desk and a four-foot wall covered in sticky notes. It didn't fit. "No way. She's on my side. She's been helping me this whole time." Aside from slamming the door in my face, anyway. But she'd get over that.

"Helping you with what, exactly? How are you going to get over this 'on the run' thing?"

"I don't know anymore. There's this other woman—"

"Another woman," Domingo said, as if that explained everything.

I snorted. Unlike him, all of my problems were not of the curvy female persuasion. "This other woman is a witch. She said that she could speak to the dead, so Suzy helped me find her. But Isobel's a fraud. That was a waste of time."

A grin. "Isobel."

"What?"

"I know that tone of voice. Can't get her off your mind?"

Of course I couldn't. She had lied to me, convinced me that she could be the solution to my problems. And she wasn't. But the sight of her standing at the top of the stairs with haunted eyes, pleading with me, asking me to let her help… That was going to stick with me for days. "It doesn't matter. I don't have a plan anymore." I ran both hands through my hair, sinking deeper into the couch. "I'm wasted—I can't even think anymore."

Domingo set down his beer, pulled out his phone. "That's why you're here. Leave the thinking to me. What do you need to get done?"

Shit, I didn't even know where to start. "The SUV needs to go. It's parked a few blocks away. It belongs to the, uh, the FBI, and I pulled out the GPS tracker, but they'll still find it sooner or later."

"Consider it gone," Domingo said, typing rapidly on his phone.

"I need another car."

"Done."

A smirk crept across my face. "Really?"

"I still know people." Domingo had been legit for a couple years now—about as long as I had been working for the OPA—but when he had been bad, he'd been really, really bad. People had looked up to him. It was no surprise that he was still in touch.

"I need to know who really killed Erin," I said.

"That I can't help you with, but your new car will be here in an hour and you're welcome to help yourself to my basement. I've got some new stuff. Wanna check it out?"

Domingo didn't even need to ask.

He took me downstairs. He had completely redone the place since my last visit. The walls were paneled half in oak, half in fancy-ass wallpaper. Sugar skulls hung from the walls with candles in their eye sockets. He had a circle of power permanently imprinted on the floor and an altar as big as a bed.

I sneezed as I set foot on the bottom of the stairs.

"Damn," I said, scrubbing at my nose with my hand. "Nice."

"Been thinking about starting a coven. I thought, with Sofia out of the house…" He trailed off, gazing around the room with a lost look, as if he didn't really recognize it. She had never been a fan of the witch thing.

He had some gemstones in a bowl of salt on his altar. Judging by the fact they were directly placed in a puddle of moonlight, I was thinking he had to be infusing them. "What are you working on?" I asked, trailing my fingers through the air over the bowl. I could just make out sparks of blue and white from the corner of my eye.

"Trying to figure out a spell to help me sleep." He scrubbed a hand over his face. "Haven't been resting well ever since…you know. Brain keeps me awake. But I can't seem to get it right. Last batch made my dreams too vivid. Kept waking up screaming."

That was a real problem. Couldn't have Domingo going crazy while he waited for Sofia to get her shit together.

I skimmed his shelves, looking through the herbs. I picked out agrimony and elder root.

"Got any passionflower?" I asked.

Domingo frowned. "Why?"

"You need passionflower."

I sprinkled the herbs I'd picked out on his gemstones. The aura of magic shifted—couldn't tell you how, but it did. I'd never been real analytical about my magic. Failed chemistry in high school twice. But I instinctively understood what Domingo needed.

His eyes were shining when he stepped up to look at it. "It's perfect."

"Test it out before you thank me," I said. "Hopefully it won't make you comatose." Although it looked like he could have used a few weeks of solid sleep. Maybe going comatose wouldn't have been the worst thing for him. I kept my eyes on the infused gemstones as I asked, "How long has she been gone now?"

"A month. Every morning I wake up and think she's making breakfast downstairs just to remember all over again," Domingo said. "I've distracted myself with the basement. Pops even did the floor for me." His gesture encompassed the room. "Now the remodel's done, but Sofia's still with *him*."

"Shit, man."

He socked me in the shoulder. "Keep the bitch eyes to yourself. Take whatever you want."

I took another pass around the shelves, looking for finished products rather than herbs. Domingo had been making poultices, too. I grabbed a bowl of strength he'd brewed and sniffed. My sinuses tingled, but no sneeze—he'd never been as good at poultices as I was. "I'm gonna take all of these. I've been away from mine a couple of days and feeling weak."

"Whatever you want," he repeated.

I stuffed my pockets with strength poultices, a few potions in plastic bottles, anything that looked vaguely useful. When I was done, I weighed an extra fifteen pounds. Or maybe that was just the exhaustion hitting me hard.

"Can I sleep in the guest room?" I asked. "Just for a few minutes."

"Why not?" Domingo agreed. "I'll make dinner happen while you nap. No shimmying down trees while I'm distracted, though—you need to get some real rest. And I'll know you've ducked out on me."

"Hey, if it worked on Pops…"

"Don't even. What do you want for dinner? Pizza? Burgers?"

"You could give me your moldy leftovers and I'd be the happiest man alive."

Domingo snorted as he pulled out his cell phone. "Not with the way I cook."

It felt like it'd been days since I smiled. I patted him on the back. He smiled back.

It was good to be home.

CHAPTER FIFTEEN

I DIDN'T SHIMMY DOWN the tree outside the guest room, but I also didn't stay for dinner. I crawled into the shower to rinse off the dirt, tossed back a few shots of energy potions, and crept out the back door as soon as the shock of consciousness hit me.

Every minute I spent at Domingo's house was another minute begging for him to be dragged out to the desert next.

My new car was a Dodge Charger, newest model year. Bumblebee yellow with two sexy black stripes up the hood. I gave a low, appreciative whistle. Domingo's "friends" were richer than I expected. That worried me—the idea that Sofia was gone and Domingo was suddenly tight with his old contacts again. But I'd deal with that later.

I grabbed the keys out of the wheel well and booked it.

My leads were dry. Erin had been murdered two days ago and I still didn't know anything about what had happened—only that Stonecrow was a dead end and that Suzy was sick of me.

If a case was going cold, then all I needed to do was heat it up. And we have a saying at my office: "There's nowhere hotter than Helltown."

The agents weren't talking about the weather when they said that. Helltown is just another neighborhood in Los Angeles, much like Chinatown, and it enjoys the same temperate winters and steamy summers that the rest of the city does.

But if you're looking for a murderer, or missing evidence, or a stolen item on the black market—chances are real good that you would find it in Helltown.

You just had to know where to look.

I drove around until sunrise, then parked the Charger at a Walmart and walked three blocks east. I stood outside Helltown with my arms folded, eyeballing the empty street in front of me.

It didn't look like anything special—definitely not a demon hideaway. From the outside, all I could see were rows of uniform housing with barred windows and sunbaked lawns. The fact that I was seeing those houses at all meant I was allowed to enter. Meant that someone inside of Helltown was expecting me.

Most humans weren't going to stumble into Helltown by accident. It was drenched in enough wards and diversion spells to render the average mortal stupid. There were lots of accidents on the intersections outside because people drove too close and got zapped with old magic. But I walked right up to the edge of the block and didn't get turned away. My invitation was open.

Not the most cheerful thought.

I stepped over the line in the sidewalk—and got smacked in the eye with a femur.

"Jesus," I growled, slapping it away, spinning to look at what I'd walked into.

From this side, I could see that the entrance to Helltown was marked with an iron arch that had bones dangling down the middle, kind of like Isobel's beaded curtains. I rubbed my face hard where the bone had touched it.

Lord, I hope the sun's bleached all the bacteria off of that.

Then I turned around to get my first look of the morning at Helltown.

As soon as I had passed under that archway, the seemingly empty street had become populated. Demons and witches and idiot humans with death wishes bustled through the road, pushing along wheelbarrows and dragging sacks behind them. The road hadn't been maintained since it vanished into Helltown in 1968, and the pavement was all but dust under my feet, making me stumble when I stepped off the sidewalk. My foot squished in something red-brown and rotting. *Graceful, Cèsar, very graceful.*

The yellowing lawns I'd seen from outside were nothing but dirt pits in here. The bars and glass were missing from most windows, letting me see to the seething darkness within the houses. All of the street signs had been torn down and replaced with sheets of engraved steel—all decorated with spikes, of course. Demons love putting spikes on *everything*.

It was a neighborhood out of a nightmare, twisted and perverse.

It was my only hope of finding a lead now.

"Welcome to Helltown," I muttered under my breath.

I was talking to myself. Three days since going rogue and I was already going nuts.

Keeping my head down, I walked fast toward the intersection of Grim and Blacksburg. Demons and witches had self-segregated within Helltown, so there are neighborhoods within the neighborhood. All the higher demons, like incubi, live on the northern streets with the mortals that feed them; I was heading south, where the less powerful demons hid out.

I never went to the north side of Helltown. *Never.*

Moving quickly, I watched my feet instead of watching my surroundings, trying to look like I belonged. I didn't want to see what I was passing anyway. The ramshackle buildings had human skulls over most doorways. Several of the houses had converted the yards to pens for exercising human servants. Vendors had carts set every few feet, selling crafts made of demon and human byproducts, selling kebabs of flesh, clothes woven from human hair. Those were the worst. Just the smell of them made me want to barf.

It wasn't a nice place, Helltown. Kopides had been trying to shut it down ever since a coven of witches and duke from the City of Dis collaborated to make those streets disappear from Los Angeles. But you can fit a lot of evil in a couple square miles, and we couldn't trust automatic weapons to operate around all that infernal power. It didn't leave a lot of options for slaughtering the residents of Helltown.

For now, the OPA only jumps in when we need something. When Helltown is spilling outside its boundaries.

As long as Helltown stays self-contained, anything goes.

Down on the south side of Helltown, there are fewer shops and more apartments. The buildings were crammed all full of demons like carcasses being eaten by maggots from the inside out. But there's one shop on the ground floor of a tenement that I've visited three or four times before. Aside from being a source of irritation for the OPA, the shopkeeper was a nosy pain-in-the-ass that always knows what's going down in her town.

Monique was one of the more innocuous demons in Helltown—a glass blower. She mostly crafted supplies for witches—vials for potion making, bowls for mixing ingredients, enchanted flasks, that kind of thing—but she also made pipes for drug use. That was the thing that got her in the most trouble. It's one thing to supply witches that live in Helltown, and another to supply potheads on the outside with pipes shaped like dicks.

Everything that demons craft gets demon energy crafted right into it. By smoking through a novelty pipe that Monique had made, druggies were opening themselves to demonic possession. It wasn't a big deal for the occasional smokers. Now imagine April twentieth at UCLA with a hundred college students that suddenly need exorcism, and you'll get why Monique is a problem.

We'd originally thought the dick-pipe affair was a witch thing, which was how it got assigned to me. Now Monique had the pleasure of being my one and only demon contact. She'd cut a deal to avoid incarceration, and she fed me information whenever I was brave enough to head into Helltown.

She still had a bunch of dick-pipes on the shelf by her front door at eye level. I had to give it to her. Monique was a real artist. Big dicks, little dicks, circumcised, uncut, all of them perfectly shaped for smoking weed.

"Get the fuck out of here," said a gravelly voice.

I dragged my attention from a nine-inch pipe with detailed veins. The artist herself was behind the counter, sitting on a stool that lifted her squat, froggy body to a normal height. She was surrounded by spindly glass sculptures. They were genuinely beautiful.

"Hey, Monique," I said. "How's business?"

She gave me a flat look. Literally a flat look. No nose, no eyebrows, barely any lips. All of her looks were flat. But this one was especially unimpressed, like I'd just asked to borrow money from her. "I've stopped selling pipes to mortal kids, so I know you're not here to fuck with me. Yet I told you to get the fuck out of here and you're not listening. You want something, you ugly cunt, so what the fuck is it this time, Hawke?"

Great. I'd caught her on a bad day. "I'm looking for information pertaining to a murder."

"You know I didn't fucking kill anyone."

I grabbed an Erlenmeyer flask off of her shelf. I could use some new equipment. "I know. You're too short to do anything worse than bite ankles."

She flashed dagger-like teeth at me. "I said I didn't kill anyone. That doesn't mean I won't."

Setting the flask on her counter, I fished around for some of the cash I'd stolen from Joey Dawes. "Erin Karwell. She was a waitress at a bar called The Olive Pit. Do you recognize the name?"

"Mortal?"

"Yeah."

"Are you sure?" Monique asked. I set a twenty on the table. Before I could let go of it, her hand shot out and seized my wrist. Her fingers were those of an artist, long and slender and delicate. Her touch sent chills rushing up my forearm. "I don't want any of your fucking money. I know why you're here. You're in deep shit, Hawke, and you're desperate for answers."

"You can't know why I'm here if you don't know Erin." I flashed the news article with her photo.

"Is that the cunt you killed?" Monique asked, barely even glancing at it.

Shit. She did know why I was there. It wasn't fun being part of Helltown's rumor mill. No fun at all. "Don't tell me you're siding with the cops on this one."

"I'm on nobody's side but mine, and my side is awfully fucking interested in not getting dead."

I pulled my hand back from her counter, twenty clutched in my fist. "Has the OPA been through here asking for me?"

"It's not the OPA you need to worry about," Monique said. "Yeah, I recognize Erin. She used to come around here."

That was news to me.

"What do you mean, 'around here?' Helltown? Your shop?"

She pushed the flask toward me. "Take it. Consider it a parting gift."

I didn't touch it. "Erin was just some waitress. What would she have been doing in Helltown?"

"Get your dumb ass down to the Temple of the Hand of Death," Monique said. "It's on Sekhmet, northwest side. That's where you'll get your answers."

My sense of alarm heightened. "Why? Is someone there expecting me?"

Her smile was even more unpleasant than her glare. "Have a nice day."

CHAPTER SIXTEEN

COMMON SENSE SAID THAT I shouldn't go to the Temple of the Hand of Death. It was on the north side. The north side of Helltown was where the incubi were, so I didn't go to the north side. Especially not if there were things expecting to see me there.

Should have been a no-brainer, right?

But common sense and desperation didn't play nicely, and I didn't have a lot of other options.

I drew my Desert Eagle before approaching the so-called temple.

It was one of the shittier buildings in Helltown. The temple looked like it occupied a former gas station, judging by the row of vintage gas pumps in front of it. You could still almost make out the graceful lines of the fifties-style decorations on the outside of the building, but they had rotted with age. The roof sagged in the middle. The sun had bleached the colors out of everything. The windows had been punched out.

Smoke spiraled out of the windows, fogging the area in front of the door. Smelled like a brushfire. I sneezed.

A steel sign had been hung over the door. It read: *"Vedae som Matis Duvak."* I didn't understand *vo-ani*, the demon language, but I was going to assume that meant "ugly-ass gas station."

I pushed the door open.

The floor inside was poured concrete. An altar stood at the far end of the room—a folding table with an array of melted candles sitting in piles of sludgy wax. There was a big clock on the wall behind it. A couple of hand-woven baskets stood along each wall. They were covered, fortunately. I didn't want to know what demons considered to be fitting offerings for demon-gods being honored in a temple gas station.

I didn't see any demons there, but I still eased the safety off the gun as I slipped inside. The door whined shut behind me.

"Is anyone here?" I asked, raising my voice. "My name is Agent Cèsar Hawke and I'm with the Office of Preternatural Affairs. I have questions."

"I have answers," someone said from behind me.

No way in hell someone had gotten behind me.

I spun to see a woman. A human woman. She had bushy brown hair, a hunched back, innocent-looking eyes. Couldn't have been any older than a gawky fifteen or sixteen. She wore black velvet—heavy skirt, sleeves that draped to her fingertips—and a boned corset. Delicate iron jewelry dangled at her neck and over her forehead. Black symbols had been painted on her cheeks, one under each eye.

She gave me a nervous smile. She was holding some kind of stone scepter that looked much too fancy for an awkward teenager.

"Are you a good man, Agent Cèsar Hawke?"

You want to talk about things that make me useless? Women were number one. Children were number two. Combine both of them by sticking a vulnerable young girl in front of me, and I turn into a giant sucker. This kid was way too young to be dressing up like an infernal priestess and hanging out in Helltown, no matter what she'd done or who she thought she was.

Every single one of my protective instincts went nuts in an instant. Like a big raging beast was trying to break out of my chest.

"Don't be afraid. I'm not going to hurt you," I said, lowering the gun. "Who are you?"

She cocked her head to the side. "Who am I? Who are *you*?"

"I'm Cèsar," I said again, slower this time, even though she'd already said my name. "What are you doing here? How did you end up in Helltown?"

Her smile turned weird. Her eyes unfocused. "I think you are probably a good man, Cèsar, but that doesn't change anything."

Wait, her eyes weren't unfocused.

They had just focused *behind* me.

I turned.

And there she was: Isobel Stonecrow, holding a folding chair in both hands like she thought she was a WWE wrestler.

She swung. The chair struck.

I was out before I hit the ground.

I didn't feel it when I went unconscious. It was like I blinked, and suddenly I was in a chair with ropes tethering my ankles and left wrist. Isobel Stonecrow was kneeling on my right side, quickly knotting the cord on that arm.

I couldn't react as quickly as I normally would have. The world was swimming around me, spinning and flipping and blurring like I'd just had another rough night with a bottle of tequila. I swiped at Isobel too slowly. By the time my fist grabbed at the place her throat had been, she had already dodged, grabbed my arm, and pinned it back to the chair.

She wasn't alone. Another priestess of the Hand of Death was behind her, watching with an amused grin that she couldn't hide behind her fingers.

Yeah, laugh it up.

"He's ridiculously handsome," the priestess said, giving Isobel a thumbs up. "Nicely done."

The corner of Isobel's mouth twitched. "Can I have a minute, Elora?"

"You can have fifteen. Or maybe twenty. However much you need." Was she waggling her eyebrows? *Jesus. Women.*

The priestess slipped past Isobel. I twisted, trying to see where she was going. I couldn't turn far. For all I knew, there were a dozen priestesses back there giggling at me really quietly.

"What the fuck, Izzy?" I asked once I was reasonably certain that we were alone.

One thick eyebrow arched, lips twisting.

"Nobody calls me Izzy."

I didn't even know why it had slipped out like that. I sure as heck wasn't feeling in a "pet names" mood with her. Probably the concussion talking.

Tried to jerk my wrist free. She had already knotted the rope. *Damn*, she was fast.

"You hang out in Helltown?" I asked as she backed away from me.

"Sometimes," Isobel said. "It's a place to settle when I'm not on the road. I have friends here."

Friends? More like coworkers. She was wearing the robes of the priestesses of the Hand of Death, all black velvet and glittering iron jewelry. I would have been lying if I said that the way the corset lifted her breasts wasn't totally awesome. But even if I'm a sucker for beautiful women—and I am—I've got my limits.

"Let me go," I said.

"All I want to do is help. Don't be afraid."

A scoff. "I'm not afraid." Not *that* afraid, anyway. But you try being held hostage by someone in Helltown without losing your cool. I'd heard stories of agents going into Helltown and never coming out again—some of them rumors, some of them definitely not. I didn't want to be another cold case. I might have been sweating a little.

Like I said, there's nowhere hotter than Helltown.

Finally prying my eyes free of Isobel in all her robes and demon jewelry, I took a long look at the room where I was now momentarily trapped. I was fairly certain that it was underneath the gas station temple. It looked like a basement. There were floorboard joists over my head. The walls were bare concrete stained with moisture. No windows. Just torches. Fucking *torches*, like we were in the Temple of Doom.

Isobel had three big baskets behind her. She grabbed one of them and hauled it closer to me.

"Let me out of here," I said.

"Not until you believe me. I'll untie you once you've seen the truth, and you can decide what to do after that."

She was still on about that? "If you're stashing kids in the temple, then what comes after that might be a call to the cops."

Isobel frowned as she dropped the basket at my feet. "Kids? You mean Ann?"

"Is that the name of your little diversion upstairs? How did she end up here? Kidnapping?"

"She's *vedae som matis bougaknati.*" Whatever the fuck *that* meant. "Don't go near Ann," Isobel said firmly. "You have to listen to me, Cèsar. I can help you. I *want* to help you."

I strained against my bindings. "Yeah, I can tell. That's why you lied to me about being able to talk to Erin and tied me to a chair."

Her eyes lit with fire. "Fine. You think I'm a fraud? Let me show you how much of a fraud I am."

She kicked over the basket. The lid flew off and hit my shins. Bones spilled out—dry human bones. I would have recoiled if I hadn't been attached to the chair.

There were no drums this time, no fake accent,

no chanting.

Isobel extended her hands over the bones in front of her, palms facing the ground. She closed her eyes.

"Come to me," she whispered.

The magic slapped me upside the head like a folding chair. My eyes burned and sinuses tingled and I sneezed three times in quick succession. The room blurred. All that magic that I had felt in at Shady Groves Cemetery was back, strong enough to choke me.

Once I could see again, all of the oxygen vanished from my lungs.

There was an apparition in front of me. The full figure of a naked, hairless human man, who looked baffled to be in the basement. His dark skin looked inhumanly gray. And—*Jesus*—I could see the basket through his shins.

He was a ghost.

His mouth moved, but Isobel spoke for him, still whispering, still in her true voice. "Where am I? What's going on?" Her eyes were empty, like the ghostly figure had taken control of her.

"Holy hell," I said.

Isobel stepped around the apparition to touch my shoulder. The ghost's empty stare followed her movements.

"Do you believe me now, Cèsar?" she asked softly.

Oh yeah. I believed her.

CHAPTER SEVENTEEN

ISOBEL HAD PARKED HER RV behind the Temple of the Hand of Death. She dragged me to it, delicate fingers encircling my wrist, eyes on the surrounding road and the creatures milling between buildings.

I must have been unconscious longer than I'd thought—it was starting to get dark by the time we left. Dangerous time to be on the streets of Helltown, even for a woman dressed like a priestess. During the day, only the corporeal, daywalking demons could go outside, making it relatively safe for visiting OPA agents. Once night fell, shit got real.

The OPA specifically forbade agents from entering Helltown in the afternoon to make sure that they wouldn't be there at nightfall.

I didn't trust a lot about the OPA right now, but I trusted their sense of self-preservation.

Isobel shoved the door to her RV open and pushed me inside. I held my breath when I stepped onto the upper step, prepared for her magic to overwhelm me. All witches have a habit of marking our territory with wards and curses, which can be enough to fuck up my nose if the witch is powerful. And Isobel was definitely powerful.

Yet I didn't sneeze. I didn't feel even the slightest tingle.

The RV looked even more retro on the inside. She had shag carpet, a beanbag chair. Her furniture was upholstered in plasticky white material. All she was missing was a lava lamp. But even though her kitchen counters were covered in jars of herbs and bags of—oh Lord, was that *blood?* I didn't see an altar.

"Don't you cast magic in here?" I asked as she climbed in behind me, slamming the door.

"Not exactly," Isobel said. She dropped the velvet skirts. They puddled around her ankles, and she kicked them away. She was wearing cutoff denim shorts underneath, which clashed with the remaining corset in a sexy kind of way.

"What's 'not exactly' supposed to mean?"

She tossed her veils to the floor and climbed into the driver's seat. "It means that I've never had a dead person in my RV, so I've never had to cast a spell in here."

The engine groaned to life and my eyebrows climbed toward my hairline. Vehicles weren't meant to work within Helltown, not with all the infernal energy. Mechanics got all gummed up. "Then how'd you get the RV working?"

"I have talented witchy friends," Isobel said, turning on the headlights. I stood behind her, hands braced on the back of her chair, as she wrenched the wheel to the right and got onto the bumpy road. "They know things."

If she knew the kind of witches powerful enough to shield her RV against infernal energy, then I wanted to know those witches, too. Heck, the entire OPA would want to know those witches. If we could bring our SUVs and BearCat assault vehicles into the neighborhood, it would change the game in a big way.

Later. After I wasn't a fugitive anymore.

"Let's get out of here," I said.

Isobel shot a smile over her shoulder at me. "You don't have to tell me twice."

The shadows were growing long, stretching in spindly fingers over the pavement. The darkness didn't have that blue cast to it that sunset often gets. It was black. Blacker than black. The shadows weren't just shadows, and they were creeping toward the RV.

The engine grumbled, floor bucking under my feet as Isobel drove toward the nearest exit.

A group of men appeared in the street. They were all narrow-shouldered and wearing studded leather jackets. They didn't walk. They sauntered, slouched, almost slithered, until they stood in the middle of the road in front of us.

Just a glance at the three of them filled my head with dirty mental images of lips and tongue and fingers. I wasn't gay or anything; everyone with a pulse would get desperately horny around these guys, and I wasn't any exception. Most humans were useless against a demon's thrall.

They were incubi. The whole reason I avoided the north side of Helltown.

Monique must have told them that she'd run into me.

"Run them over," I said.

"*What?*"

"You heard me!"

Isobel slammed on the brakes, skidding to a stop on the gravel. Her bumper stopped inches from their legs. The trio of incubi didn't even twitch.

"Are you crazy, Izzy? Don't fucking stop!"

She twisted the wheel, tried to move forward. One of the incubi stepped in front of the RV. Pressed his pale hand against the windshield.

His thrall rolled through me.

Incubi are demons that look like humans in all the ways that count. They've got faces like ours. Two arms, two legs, all the normal parts. But they don't come from Earth. They come from somewhere much hotter and darker. And they don't survive by eating food like normal people do.

They feed on sex. And they can make *anyone* desire them using their powers of thrall.

That probably sounds like a useless power, as far as demon talents go, but have you ever tried killing someone that you desperately want to fuck? Let me tell you—it's a hell of a defense.

And these guys didn't just want sex.

They wanted me dead.

Even knowing that they were out to kill us, dirty thoughts flashed through my mind. It built quickly as the incubus shoved all his demon energies at us. Naked bodies, big, long dicks, dripping pussies.

It wasn't the first time I'd faced an incubus. I knew how to break free.

We needed distance.

"Isobel, *go!*" I said.

But her eyes were glazed over, breath quickening. Her hands dropped from the steering wheel into her lap.

One of the other incubi was approaching our door.

I wanted to rip off my clothes and let him enter. Who cared if he wanted to kill us? It would be sweet, orgasmic death. I wanted to let him have me. I wanted to let him have Isobel. I wanted…

Distance.

He opened the door. I slammed it shut and locked it. Through the window, I got a great look at his jacket. I wasn't surprised to notice that it was being held shut by silver needles. That was a mark of the local incubus mafia—the gang that ruled Los Angeles and, not coincidentally, loathed my guts.

"You can't fucking have us," I said. It was hard to speak. I wasn't actually sure that the words made it out of my mouth. The thrall was turning me stupid.

Lord, I wanted him. He wasn't even attractive. Way too square. Way too *male*. But his black eyes smoldered and it took all my strength to turn away. If I kept staring, I was going to open the door for him—and I didn't want him and his silver needles to be able to reach me.

Isobel still wasn't moving. She was rubbing between her thighs, groaning softly.

At another time, that would have been a fun

distraction. But not now. "Sorry, baby," I muttered, shoving her out of the chair. She didn't even fight me as she spilled to the floor.

The other incubi were approaching the windshield now. In about five seconds, I was going to be surrounded by so many demons that I'd be helpless to the desire, just like Isobel.

So I didn't give them five seconds.

I slammed my foot on the gas.

The RV didn't have much juice behind it, especially in Helltown, but it lurched forward. I knocked into two of the incubi, who hadn't backed up fast enough. One of them fell under my wheels. The *bump* was way too satisfying.

The guy at the door ran along our side, slamming his hands into the door. I couldn't hear what he was shouting over the engine noises.

Every fiber of my being wanted to stop the RV —every fiber except that narrow sliver of self-preservation that was screaming. Stopping would mean death. So I kept my foot flat on the pedal.

The last incubus fell away. He couldn't keep up.

I swung the wheel around, turning a tight corner. The iron arch leading back to civilization appeared at the end of the street.

We passed through the barrier. My heart contracted and my sinuses itched.

The instant that we were out of Helltown's wards, Domingo's cell phone rang.

I didn't answer it. I drove faster.

The more distance I put between Helltown and me, the faster the thrall faded. It took three blocks before I could think of anything but turning back and letting our attackers have their way with me.

I dared a look over my shoulder at Isobel as I careened down the streets. "Izzy? You okay?"

She was pulling her shorts up and buttoning them, cheeks flushed bright red. "I'm fine. I think." She sat in the passenger's seat, twisted around to watch Helltown disappear through the back window.

"Are we being followed?"

"I don't see anyone," she said. She let her head drop into her hands. "I'm so sorry about that, Cèsar. That was my fault. I never should have gone back to *vedae som matis duvak*—they were probably watching for my RV."

"Wait, what? Why would the incubi be after you? I thought they were after me."

She frowned. "Huh?"

Interesting. It seemed we had a mutual enemy. "Not a friend of the Silver Needles?"

Isobel stuffed her breasts back into her corset.

"No," she said flatly.

Domingo's phone rang again, interrupting us. This time, I answered it. "Domingo here."

It was Suzy. "You still in LA, Cèsar?"

I had never been happier to hear her voice before. I didn't bother asking how she knew that I had my brother's cell phone. Suzy knew everything. "I thought you were done with me."

"I've come to terms with the fact that you're not leaving town until you've got your answers. So you want to talk to Erin Karwell or not?"

"You found her."

"I'm breaking about fifty laws that most

Americans don't even know exist to tell you this. I could lose my job. I could be imprisoned. I could be *killed*. I hope you're grateful."

"Oh, I'm grateful. I could just about kiss you," I said.

Isobel gave me a side eye. I ignored her and kept driving.

"Don't go all sappy on me." But Suzy's voice had softened. "Her body wasn't taken to the usual morgue. She was sent to Bittman Labs, out in Torrance."

Torrance? That wasn't anywhere near the scene of the crime. But I knew where it was, so I got into the turn lane. "I owe you, Suze."

"Hell yeah, you do." A pause, and then, "Do you still have the necrocog?"

"She's with me right now."

Isobel gave me another look, this one more warning. The same kind of look Aunt Raina used to give me before beating sense into my ass with a chancla.

"I guess that's good," Suzy said. "I'm going to meet you at Bittman Labs. I'm on my way now."

"Don't. You've gotten yourself in enough danger."

"Did it sound like I was asking for your opinion? I'll meet you around back in, what, half an hour? Maybe forty-five. Don't go in without me."

Suzy hung up the phone.

"Who was that?" Isobel asked, a hard edge to her voice.

"Suzume Takeuchi. Suzy. The woman we visited."

"Your coworker at the Office of Preternatural Affairs? The place that's sending guys out to *execute* us?"

"That has nothing to do with Suzy."

"Are you so sure about that?" When I stopped at the intersection, Isobel grabbed my arm, forcing me to look at her. "If someone in the OPA is out to get you, how do you know that you can trust anyone that works there?"

Eduardo and Joey *were* friends of Suzy's. But I shook off the thought as soon as it crept over me. A lot of crazy shit had happened the last few days, but if I could trust anything, it was my taste in friends. "You don't know Suzy," I said. Isobel made a noncommittal sound in the back of her throat. That sound was enough to take me from offended to pissed in two seconds flat. "How do I know I can trust *you*? You're the one fucking around with demons in Helltown."

"I'm the one the incubi in Helltown want dead," she said dryly.

I winced. "Good point. The enemy of my enemy, or…whatever."

"She's been in Helltown," Isobel said.

"What? Who?"

"Your Suzy. I asked around. Does she usually wear business suits and throw money at all her contacts? She was in Helltown this morning. Yesterday, too."

That was news to me. But it didn't mean anything. Suzy had multiple cases, just like I usually did. She could have been chasing down anyone. "We can trust Suzy."

A smile flickered over Isobel's lips. "I hope so, because you're staking both of our lives on it."

The light turned green. We got on the freeway and headed for Torrance.

CHAPTER EIGHTEEN

THERE WAS ONLY ONE car in the parking lot when we got to Bittman Labs, and it wasn't Suzy's. Isobel passed the building at a crawl, leaning forward to squint out the windshield. "Is that hers?" she asked.

"No, Suzy said she'd be around back."

Isobel hesitated, knuckles white on the steering wheel. "Last chance to escape with our lives."

"I won't have a life if we leave," I said.

She parked the RV behind the morgue.

Suzy was already waiting for us on foot. No car in sight. She gave me a look through the windshield that could have curdled milk—or maybe that look was for the giant teal beast that came groaning around the corner.

I jumped out.

"Hey, Scooby," Suzy said by way of greeting. "Nice Mystery Machine. Why is your bumper bloody?"

It was Isobel who responded from behind me. "It's incubus blood. Don't worry about it." She clambered out of the RV, pulling a t-shirt over the corset that had more holes than cloth in it. The Cabo Wabo logo was stretched over her ample breasts.

Suzy's expression changed completely as she looked Isobel up and down, hand resting almost casually on her hip where she usually wore a holster. No gun tonight. Probably for the best. The two of them together were a real Odd Couple, all right—Suzy buttoned up tight in a suit and tie, Isobel fast and loose.

"Agent Takeuchi," Suzy said, extending her hand. "We haven't officially met yet." It was hard to tell what she was thinking, but the vein that had appeared in her forehead made me think it wasn't real good.

After a beat, Isobel shook her hand. "I'm Isobel Stonecrow." Was that a moment of hesitation before she said her name? Man, I wanted to run her face through our databases. See what other pseudonyms she might have.

"Why is there incubus blood on your RV?"

Suzy didn't know about my history with the Silver Needles, and I didn't want to have to explain why incubi might be attacking me. When Isobel opened her mouth to reply, I interrupted her. "We can talk later. We're in kind of a rush with Erin now, aren't we?" I asked.

"I guess so," Suzy said. "Where are your supplies for the spell, Stonecrow?"

Isobel glanced at me.

I answered for her. "She doesn't need them."

"But the ritual sites we've found…"

"Fake," I said.

"Interesting." I'd seen Suzy in a lot of weird moods before, but not this one. She was usually brash. Aggressive. But this chilly thing, this was new. She jerked a thumb toward the back door. "I called ahead. Rob left it unlocked. Just gotta go in."

She turned and headed inside.

Isobel hung back, hesitating to follow.

"Problem?" I asked.

"This is going to sound like the obvious statement of the day, but there are a lot of dead bodies in there."

And she could probably hear every last one of them. I wouldn't be eager to go inside either. "Could you call up Erin from out here?"

"I need to be closer than that."

But she didn't look like she was in a hurry to make that happen.

Suzy opened the back door, propping it against her foot so that it stayed open. "Coming?"

"I'm coming," Isobel said, but she still didn't move.

"I don't like morgues," I said. "You got my back on this?" I reached out for her, offering a hand. She stared at me for a long time before taking it.

"Sure," she said, leaning against my side. We fit together pretty well. "I've got your back."

I'd like to say that was just a smooth line to get her inside, but not so much. Never been a fan of morgues. Bodies give me the heebie jeebies.

Suzy held the door until we passed through. Then she closed it, punched a few numbers in the keypad by the handle, reactivated the alarm sensors by pressing a red button.

We were in a sterile hallway. The night crew wasn't in this part of the building, so only the emergency signs over the doors gave us any light.

Suzy clicked on a penlight and traced it along the wall. "Rob said he'd leave me alone to check the bodies, but I didn't tell him that I'd have company. Be quiet."

"What excuse did you give him for wanting a little one-on-one time with cadavers?" I asked in a whisper.

"I didn't give him an excuse. I gave him money." Suzy led us down an adjacent hall. Isobel had pulled back from me, hugging her arms around herself, walking slowly. She was shivering in her shorts and tee.

Shucking my jacket, I dropped it over her shoulders. I had long sleeves underneath. It didn't make a difference to me. But she looked startled and kind of pleased. "Thanks," she said, pulling the lapels closed over her chest.

"I looked up Peter's case file," Suzy said, walking backward so that she could address me directly. She talked like Isobel wasn't with us. "Our last necrocog."

"I remember Peter."

"They scanned his personal notes and put them in the database. Good reading. Did you know the dead can't lie?"

"Of course they can't," Isobel said, picking up her pace to walk alongside me. "Souls move on after the bodies are gone. All that they leave is residue. An imprint. Memories don't have the motivation to lie. The testimony of the dead is inviolable."

Suzy nodded. "If the victim's body is still here, and if Stonecrow can talk to her, you'll have your answer." She stopped in front of the door to the refrigerator and gave me a hard look. "You sure you want that? It's not too late for you to hop a bus to Mexico."

I answered by pushing the door open.

It was even colder inside. One wall was nothing but silver drawers. There was a steel table in the middle, some jars and cabinets to the wall on the right. Chills rolled down my spine at the sight of them.

Suzy grabbed a clipboard off the wall. "Karwell, Karwell…" she muttered, tracing her flashlight down the page.

While she searched for Erin's name, Isobel moved to stand in front of the drawers. She'd been reluctant to enter the building, but she didn't look reluctant now. She looked…drunk. Intoxicated. Her eyes were lidded and she was breathing heavy.

"Isobel?"

She didn't respond to me. She lifted her hands in front of her like she was trying to push curtains apart.

That glazed look was starting to freak me out. Way creepier than tribal drums and raccoon bones and shit.

Suzy hung the clipboard up on the wall again and faced me. Her features were pinched. Bad sign. "Erin Karwell is here."

"Where?"

She didn't move toward the drawers. She went

to the cabinets on the opposite wall, grabbed keys hanging from a hook, and unlocked them. There were several white boxes inside, each a bit smaller than a banker's box. Isobel recoiled at the sight of them.

Suzy grabbed one. I'd be lying if I said I didn't take a few steps back when she carried it over and set it on the steel table.

She lifted the top. There was a bag of gray dust inside.

Cremains.

"Erin Karwell," she said.

CHAPTER NINETEEN

I'D FLIRTED WITH ERIN for months, so you'd think that I would know more about her. Or at least be able to put together a memory of her face and hold it clear in my mind, as crisp as the grayscale photograph in my pocket. Like, what color were her eyes? Were her ears pierced? Did she wear jewelry?

I couldn't remember any of that without checking the picture Domingo had printed up. I couldn't remember Erin's smile or laugh or even her black eye all that well. Months of heavy tipping and one trip sneaking into the kitchen to find her name, and I couldn't even tell you how long her hair had been when she wasn't wearing a ponytail.

But I remembered what her body looked like in my bathtub. I remembered her cracked fingernail and the hole between her breasts. I remembered the bruised shape of a hand imprinted on her unbreathing throat.

Now even that was gone.

Erin Karwell had been cremated. Body vaporized.

"Shit," I said. "I'm *fucked*." Probably an understatement.

Suzy seemed to deflate. It didn't look like disappointment, but relief. "Guess that's it," she said, moving to put the lid back onto the box.

Isobel stopped her by reaching in to grab the plastic bag. "I can try. I've never done ash before, but I've worked with some rotted bodies. It can't be that different."

"A lot of cremains are just bone and whatever the victim was burned inside," Suzy said, her voice hard-edged as she tried to pull the box out of Isobel's reach. "There's probably barely any of the body left."

Isobel dragged the bag toward her anyway. "We can at least attempt it."

They were playing tug of war with the box. I settled it by grabbing Erin's cremains and placing them in front of Isobel. She pulled the rubber band off, folded down the edges of the bag.

"Cèsar," Suzy said warningly.

"The worst thing that can happen is nothing," I said. "Stop worrying so much."

"It can be so much worse than that," she whispered. I ignored her.

Isobel had her hands stretched out over the cremains and her eyes had gone blank. She stared at the wall without seeming to see it. "Erin Karwell? Erin...come on..." Her cheeks flushed. The muscles in her hands strained.

I felt her voice all the way down in my stomach. *Erin Karwell...*

Magic built around us, pressing tight inside my

chest as silvery mist lifted from the cremains. I smothered my nose and mouth with a hand, fighting not to sneeze at the force of magic.

Erin didn't appear as quickly as the man in the temple had. I glimpsed ghostly legs, but they faded to nothing within moments. Then I glimpsed a sliver of face. Eyes without irises. A bald scalp.

The body formed slowly, painstakingly, blurred around the edges.

There she was. Erin.

Suzy stepped back, reflexively reaching for the pistol she wasn't carrying again.

Erin looked down at herself, running ghostly hands over her breasts. They looked smaller than I thought I remembered. Maybe she'd had implants and plastic surgery hadn't translated to her ghost. The hair wasn't there either, just like it hadn't been on the man Isobel had raised. She looked bald.

The ghost flickered. Her legs had never fully formed. When I stepped to the left, I could see that she didn't have a back either, more like a flat picture than an entire body.

Guess cremains were enough to summon her soul, but only barely.

Her mouth moved. Isobel spoke for her.

"What's going on?" she asked softly.

It was quiet in the morgue. Dead quiet. No pun intended. Isobel was whispering, but I didn't have to strain my ears to hear her at all.

"Erin?" I said.

Isobel grimaced, pressed a hand to her forehead. The ghost vanished for a full second before reappearing. "Where am I?" Erin asked through Isobel. "What happened?"

"My name is Agent Takeuchi. I'm with the Federal Bureau of Investigation." Suzy sounded hoarse, kind of freaked out, but I still almost laughed at her introducing herself as a member of the FBI. Like a dead woman was really going to ruin our cover. "I need to ask you a few questions. Can you hear me?"

Erin nodded. Her gaze drifted over the room, but just like Isobel, she didn't seem to see any of it.

Was it really her? Was it her soul manifesting, or some faint residue still imprinted in her cremains?

"What's the last thing you remember, Miss Karwell?" Suzy asked.

Isobel spoke. "I went to work. I was running late." She flinched, mouth twisting and brow furrowing. "I went to work. I was running late. I've been running late a lot, so Thandy chewed me out." She groaned and bent over at the waist as if someone had struck her. At the same time, Erin faded out of view then faded back. "I went to work," Isobel whimpered. "I was running late."

Damn. Erin was barely there. I wanted to grab Isobel, shake her free of the connection, but stood frozen at the end of the table. I needed to hear this. I needed to get past Thandy to what happened after that.

The door opened. An out-of-breath morgue tech rushed in, and stopped short at the sight of the ghost. "Praise Allah," he breathed.

"Rob," Suzy said, stepping toward him, trying to block his view. It was too late. He'd already seen her. "Get out of here. I told you to leave us alone. I fucking *paid* you."

His mouth worked soundlessly. "It's—the—what is that?"

"Rob. What are you doing here?"

"The cops," he said. Erin was reflected in his wide eyes. "The cops are here. I know the alarms are disabled, and I didn't call them, so someone must have…tipped them off…" He tried to move toward Erin's blurry ghost. "Is that a ghost?"

Suzy swore in a language that wasn't English. "I'll take care of this," she told me, seizing Rob's arm, dragging him into the hallway. She left the door open. I could watch their shadows slide over the wall as she hauled ass toward the reception desk. Voices I didn't recognize echoed back toward me.

We were out of time.

"Keep Erin here," I urged Isobel. "Just a few more seconds."

The sound of my voice finally drew Erin's attention to me. Her ghost solidified and brightened. Her blank eyes penetrated me.

"Cèsar?" she asked through Isobel's mouth.

"Yeah," I said. "Yeah, baby. It's me. I'm here. You gotta tell me who killed you. I need to know what happened."

Her glowing, delicate hands flew to her throat. Erin's white eyes widened and her mouth opened.

Isobel began to scream.

Shit.

I grabbed her wrists, shoved her away from Erin's ashes. Didn't help. Isobel was trapped. All tangled up in Erin's spirit.

And there was no fucking way that the cops wouldn't hear it.

Footsteps beat in the hallway. I heard Suzy shout.

I shook Isobel hard. "Let go! We have to run!"

"You killed me!" she shrieked, beating at my chest, trying to wrench free. "*You killed me*!"

What she was saying sunk in. The room spun around me. Erin's horrified mirage clutched at her heart where the bullet wound had been, screaming through Isobel's lips as she stared at me, fraying around the edges. The ghost vanished with terror in her eyes, and Isobel kept screaming.

Terror pounded through me. The cops were still fighting with Suzy in the hall and getting closer. We needed to be gone. *Now*.

I lifted Isobel off of her feet, slammed her back into the wall.

"*Izzy!*"

Her scream cut off, mouth still open, eyes blank.

Slowly, she focused on me.

"Nobody calls me Izzy," she whispered. She reached up to touch my face. Her fingers brushed along my jaw, up my cheekbones, to my brow, like she was identifying my features with her hands. "Oh my God, Cèsar. Oh my *God*."

She didn't have to tell me what she had learned from her connection to Erin. I already knew what she was going to say.

I had killed Erin Karwell.

CHAPTER TWENTY

SOMEHOW, WE ESCAPED. DON'T even fucking ask how, because I don't know.

Everything went from screaming to running in about two seconds flat. There had been gunshots. Suzy had been yelling, flashing her badge. Men had shoved guns in my face and grabbed my sleeves. I had punched someone. Maybe a couple someones.

Then Isobel and I had been running. We'd gotten into her RV. And then we were driving.

After that, all I knew was that we ended up outside Los Angeles. It was night outside the windows. Desert stretched to the hills. We weren't on a road anymore. We were far from the LAPD, far from the OPA, far from Suzy at the morgue.

But there was no running from what I had learned.

I sat on Isobel's creaky futon and stared at my hands. They looked bigger than usual. I wondered if the shape of them matched the dark imprints on Erin's throat before her body had been reduced to nothing but ash. I hadn't checked. I'd been too busy freaking out. I hadn't believed it could have been me anyway.

I still couldn't believe it.

"Erin." Her name was a prayer on my lips. An apology.

I wasn't that guy. I wasn't someone who got drunk enough to black out. I wasn't capable of getting drunk enough to shoot a woman.

And yet, somehow, I was.

Like Suzy had said, the dead couldn't lie.

You killed me, she'd said. *You killed me*. God, those screams. They'd carved my heart right out of my chest and left me hollow on the inside.

Isobel stood a few feet in front of me. Just out of arm's reach. She was staring at me as if seeing my face for the first time. She wasn't driving, so that meant that the RV had stopped at some point. I wasn't sure when.

"Did you lie to me?" she asked.

I didn't understand the question. "What?"

"You told me that you didn't kill Erin. Were you lying to me?"

She had heard what Erin had said, hadn't she? She knew what I had done. I could see it in her face. "I didn't know," I said slowly. "I didn't think that I would have ever done…that. I wasn't lying to you. I believed that to be true."

"I don't think I want you in my RV."

I couldn't blame her for that. I stood.

She pushed me back onto the futon.

"I didn't tell you to leave," she said. I stared up at her blearily, trying to understand. "We're miles out of town. There's nowhere for you to go anyway.

So don't even think about bailing on me."

That was a lot of sympathy for a murderer.

I leaned back against the wall, stared up at the ceiling. "I should have turned myself in to the OPA."

She sat next to me. The mattress sagged under our combined weight. She touched my leg and I pulled away.

Erin wasn't going to smile again, never serve drinks again, and I'd ended that. It was *me*.

"I should really go," I said. I could barely hear my own voice over the roar of shock in my ears. High blood pressure, probably. My adrenaline was still insane. I felt cold all over.

"Go where?"

"Just…go." To the desert. Find that ditch where we'd abandoned Joey and Eduardo. Climb in, pull the dirt over me, never climb out again. It would still be better than I deserved.

Isobel slid her arm around my back. "You're not going anywhere like this, Cèsar."

How could she touch me, knowing what we knew now?

"I killed her," I said.

A shadow flashed through Isobel's eyes. She brushed the hair off of my forehead. "She didn't come back right. The cremains were harder to work with than I thought. She didn't really know what she was saying." She looked thoughtful. "I really thought that it should have worked with her remnants like that. I'm not sure why it didn't. If it wasn't so dangerous to go back to Helltown, I'd ask Ann what she thinks, but…"

But the incubi there were watching for us now.

Maybe I should have let the Silver Needles have me.

"I'm not a real witch," Isobel said. She was changing the subject to something easier to stomach than murder. Fine.

Dully, I said, "I just watched you raise Erin."

"Yeah, but that's all I can do. I told you that I didn't enchant my RV's engine—that was something my friend did for me as a favor because I *can't*. I've never cast a spell in here because I don't have whatever it takes. I can't do wards. I can't even light a candle."

"The blister powder," I said.

"Another present from my friend."

"The cure?"

"Those are just herbs that counter the effects. It's not magic." Isobel shrugged. "I am a fraud—just not the way you thought. I have to fake my rituals because I can't cast spells for anything."

"Why are you telling me this?"

"I'm coming clean with you," she said gently. "As clean as I get with anyone. I want you to know…I trust you. No matter what happened with Erin, I trust that you're a good guy."

"Don't," I said.

Isobel touched my wrist. "I've met a lot of bad people before, Cèsar. I've known career criminals. Not people who hurt by accident, but people who hurt by design, and those who enjoy it. You're not one of those people."

But I was. I had killed Erin.

Lord, the fear in her eyes when she looked at

me…

"You're right. You killed Erin Karwell. But that doesn't make you a bad man," Isobel said. "I know you're not with the Needles. And come on, you were more worried about the safety of a teenager hiding out at the Temple of the Hand of Death than you were about being held captive. That's not something bad men worry about. I've seen the goodness in you."

"That another one of your witch powers?"

She smiled faintly. "I don't need magic to know goodness when I see it, Cèsar."

"You shouldn't even be sitting next to me."

She rubbed her thumb over my knuckles. "You won't hurt me."

I wanted to believe that was true. I wanted it to be true so badly that it hurt deep down on the inside. "I always thought that…" It was too hard to get the words out. It felt like I was choking on Erin's name, like she had become permanently lodged in my chest. "You know why those incubi wanted me dead?" Dumb question. Of course she didn't. But she was polite enough to shake her head. "It was because I saved my sister, Ofelia. That's what made me an OPA agent, too. Saving Ofelia." Like that could change what I'd done to Erin.

"What happened to her?" Isobel asked.

It was a question I'd gotten a few times before, from a few different people. I'd never answered it before. It wasn't anyone's business.

But fate, destiny, whatever, had entrusted Isobel with the testimony of the dead. She had followed me into a morgue to try to clear my name. She hadn't run when she'd learned the truth.

If I could trust anyone, it was Isobel.

So I told her.

CHAPTER TWENTY-ONE

SOUNDS CLICHÉ TO SAY it, but it was a dark and stormy night. The kind of night where the wind blows the trees sideways and tosses the ocean against the beach like it's got a vendetta against the sand. It was Hurricane Raquel, a should-have-been-impossible tempest ravaging California.

All the sane people were hiding indoors. But my sister had still been out there somewhere. Nobody had seen her for days. Her last text message had been to Domingo, asking him to pick her up at the CVS a few blocks from her house, but she hadn't been there when he'd arrived.

It wasn't all that weird. Ofelia was a hurricane all her own. She had a habit of flaking out and disappearing with friends for days only to return later in a whole new outfit with her head shaved, a new tattoo, and dark rings under her eyes. That was normal for Ofelia.

But this wasn't normal. She'd been running with new friends. Instead of coming back from outings with tattoos, she was coming back with caked-on makeup that almost entirely concealed bruises. And now the hurricane had moved in and she hadn't talked to anyone, not even Pops.

So I'd tracked her. Hacked into her Find My Phone account and zeroed in on the GPS. I wasn't working for the OPA then—I was a private dick, paying my rent by catching vanishing parolees and taking photos of cheating spouses. I didn't have access to any of the databases that I would later on. Searching for her phone was as fancy as I could get.

It was good enough. In a few minutes, I had an answer.

Ofelia's phone had been dropped outside the gates to Helltown.

At the time, I didn't know what it was. The neighborhood just looked like a piece of shit to me. One big gray blight on the face of Los Angeles. It didn't occur to me that the cars and houses were just illusions.

I looked around for her phone and couldn't find it on the street.

When I turned around, I saw people appear out of that empty road. They shimmered when they crossed the invisible barrier. It was a group of three slender men with long black hair, all wearing leather, all pale-skinned and perfect. And they'd come out of fucking nowhere.

I ducked into an alley, heart jackhammering, and watched.

The men melted halfway into the shadows while they talked. They didn't look human because they weren't. Abuelita had taught me to cast magic, but this? This was new. It was the first I'd seen of this world, a place filled with demons and haunts and things that bumped in the night.

One of them was holding something.

Ofelia's phone.

I thought about attacking them right there. Oh man, did I want to attack. They had seen my sister. They knew where to find her. But I understood instinctively that they weren't human and that throwing a few punches wouldn't do shit to stop them.

Before I figured out what to do, they climbed into an Audi parked on the corner and drove off.

I wouldn't figure out what I had seen for days, not until I was working for the OPA and Fritz Friederling debriefed me. But I can tell you now that they were incubi. They'd been coming out of Helltown.

At the time, all I knew was this: They had Ofelia's phone.

So I got in my car and followed them.

They went to a beach house in this insane hurricane. It was built up on stilts. All the sand had been washed out from under it, but the house stood strong in the storm.

One of the incubi got out of the car. Went into the house. Then the car left.

I had to climb up and break a window to follow him inside. Looked like a normal vacation home. Any kind of place you would have found on a B&B website, pretty much. Generic furniture, generic wallpaper. Non-smoking signs.

But there was a glass bowl in the kitchen. That bowl was filled with needles as long as my fingers and sharper than knives.

I hadn't known it at the time, but that was the calling card of the Silver Needles—the incubus mafia.

The man I'd followed was in the bathroom washing up. He was shirtless, covered in tattoos from his waist to his neck. There was an eagle inked on his spine. Its wings wrapped around his throat, touched his chin. Ofelia's phone was on the sink next to him.

I slipped past him. Headed up into the attic. Not sure how I knew I'd find her there, but I did.

Ofelia was hogtied in the corner. There was a ball gag in her mouth. There was so much blood on her face and neck that I barely even recognized her.

She tried to speak around the gag and couldn't. I peeled it out of her mouth. "Ofelia?"

My baby sister said, "Cèsar," and then she began to sob.

When I untied her, I realized she was fully dressed. No torn clothes. Same outfit she'd disappeared in. All the wounds were on her face and neck and hands. They hadn't touched her anywhere else. But her cheeks, her lips, her eyelids —they were riddled with tiny punctures.

The demons had used that bowl of needles on her.

She told me what had happened as I untied her. Turned out that the Silver Needles, despite being sex demons, didn't rape their victims. They were the sickest kind of sadists—the kind that got off on psychological pain as much as the physical kind. They enjoyed the process of forcing people to give themselves up, so they didn't use thrall to coerce anyone. They liked the victims to beg for sex.

The Needles gave their captives two choices: get tortured, or consent to being fucked to death. "Willing" demon food.

Ofelia had picked torture.

So they'd tortured her. Lord, had they tortured her. But Ofelia had held out.

She'd been at the mercy of the Needles for a week. An entire fucking *week*. They'd ripped her so full of holes that she was faint from blood loss, and she hadn't given in.

I thought about the incubus washing up in the bathroom, the bowl of needles in the kitchen.

I thought about killing him.

But Ofelia was too weak to walk. I tossed her over my shoulder and climbed out of the attic like that.

I took her straight to the hospital. I stuck by her side the whole time that the nurses were bandaging her wounded body, and when the cops showed up to question her. She refused to file a police report. She told me that it'd just get the cops killed if they went after her attacker—he wasn't human; they couldn't hurt him.

So once she fell asleep, I went back to get the fucker that had taken her myself.

He was still at the beach house. I found him talking on Ofelia's cell phone under the pier. He looked agitated. Fearful. He was telling someone on the other end that he'd lost her and that the Needles were going to kill him for it. His eagle tattoo jutted over his collar, so I could tell that it was the same guy, and the sight of him made my vision go red.

I interrupted his call by smashing his head into the rocks.

Saying what I did to him wouldn't make me sound good. I'm not a violent guy, you know. When I arrested witches on the OPA's most wanted list, I'd rather sneak up on them than risk a direct confrontation. But this guy, I just about knocked his fucking head off.

He never saw me coming.

That was how I discovered that incubi have a weakness—a big one. When they bleed, they bleed *hard*. His skull cracked when I dropped him. He poured blood all over the sand. And I realized that I might have gotten what I'd been fantasizing about, but didn't really want—I might have actually killed the guy.

I used Ofelia's phone to call for an ambulance. Fucking stupid, right? An ambulance for the demon from Hell.

I didn't get EMTs. I got black SUVs.

The guy who came out on the beach to greet me had blond hair and a nice suit and a look of surprise. He asked me if I'd tracked and taken down the incubus on my own. I told him yes. And I apologized. I felt like shit for what I'd done to the incubus. I wanted him to face justice, not die.

Apparently, that was the right thing to say. The blond man smiled at me. He told me that his name was Fritz Friederling, and he didn't arrest me.

He asked me if I wanted a job.

"So did he die?"

I looked at Isobel for the first time. I'd been staring at her beaded curtains the whole time I talked. Didn't want to have to see what she thought of me. But now I saw, and she was watching me with sympathy in her eyes.

"Fritz said that he was locked up in a Union detention facility," I said. "So, yes, he survived."

"And Ofelia?"

"She healed. Just about disowned me for going after the incubus on my own, but she's fine. Back to her usual shit. Getting into trouble." I couldn't help but smile to think of her. She was getting in trouble in Mexico now, somewhere with warm beaches and no incubus mafia.

"Sounds like you did all the right things," Isobel said.

It was the first time I'd told anyone the whole story since starting to work for the Office of Preternatural Affairs. And she didn't think I was stupid or a violent animal. My heart unclenched a little.

"Fritz probably saved my life from retaliation by the Needles," I said. "The job's good. I love my job. And I've ruined all of it." I gave her a sideways look. "Why did you think the incubi were out to kill you?"

She looked surprised by the question. "Oh. It's just…Helltown drama, I guess. North side versus south side. Death's Hand doesn't like incubi and vice versa. They're always after the priestesses."

"I don't think you should go back there."

Isobel stroked her fingernails through my hair.

"I can take care of myself."

I was too exhausted to argue. I dropped my head into my hands again. "I wasn't lying to you when I told you I didn't kill Erin. I didn't know—I never thought I could have—"

She kissed me.

My first reaction was all animal—the little brain, not the big brain. She climbed into my lap and all I could think about was how incredible she felt, the way she tasted, the smell of her hair. She pushed me so that my back bumped the wall and she kissed hard.

I liked it. A lot.

But big brain won out. I grabbed her by the arms instead of the parts I really wanted to grab. I pushed her back.

She looked surprised and confused. "What?"

"What do you think you're doing?"

Isobel skimmed her fingernail down my cheek, like she was tracing the path of a tear. I tried not to look down her shirt. It was hard. I had a great view from that angle. "I've been thinking about kissing you ever since you saved me in the desert. Actually, that's a lie. I've been thinking about it ever since I washed your face off and realized you weren't a hideous gargoyle."

I was too confused to be offended. "But I killed Erin."

"Oh, Cèsar," she sighed, like I was totally clueless. She melted against my chest. Her head felt good tucked against my neck. "You need to turn yourself in. Tell Fritz everything that's happened—everything about the Needles in Helltown, and

Erin Karwell, and the Union guys. I know he'll be able to help you."

"Turn myself in?"

"Yes. I'll take you to him in the morning."

So Isobel wasn't afraid of me, but she still thought I should be arrested. She was probably right. That was the only way that Erin Karwell was going to get the justice she deserved now.

But I couldn't let Isobel drive me to Fritz's house. The OPA had been looking for her. They wouldn't just arrest me.

"You're right," I said. "I'll turn myself in. And I should probably—"

Isobel put her hand over my mouth. "Shut up and hold me."

That I could do.

I wrapped my arms around her. Lord, what I would have given to have been with a woman like Isobel a week ago. Before I hurt Erin. Before I fucked up and made an innocent life pay for it.

Isobel didn't try to kiss me again. She rested against me, warm and comfortable and silent, giving me the trust I didn't deserve.

Eventually, her breathing slowed. She relaxed.

I'd had energy potions, but Isobel hadn't. She probably hadn't slept in days. Made it easy to gently move her off of me, stretching her out on the cot. Took superhuman strength not to lie down next to her, but I didn't. I grabbed another energy potion out of my jacket, took a quick swig.

Then I went walking.

CHAPTER TWENTY-TWO

I HAD TO WALK for three hours before I finally spotted a cab. The closest things I had to water were the energy and strength potions I'd snagged from Domingo, so I drank them as I walked up the highway toward Los Angeles. I was jittering hard by the time I got into the checkered cab.

"Where to?" the cabbie asked me.

My hands were shaking like I'd tossed back a twelve pack of Red Bull. I raked my fingers through my hair. I was soaked with sweat.

It wasn't just the walk or the potions. It was knowing what I had to do next.

For a second, I thought about telling him to take me back to Isobel. I thought about locking myself in the RV with her and seeing what else she'd been thinking about doing to me. I thought about asking her how she felt about spending the summer in Mexico with Ofelia, maybe heading into Guatemala to visit Abuelita's family.

But Isobel wouldn't take me back, so I gave him a different address.

The driver turned on the meter and got on the

road.

Fritz Friederling lived in Beverly Hills. He'd told me over drinks at The Pit once that his great-grandfather had been big in mining—something about minerals—and Fritz had inherited everything when he was sixteen. He worked for the OPA because he was passionate about keeping the country safe, not because he wanted the benefits. Definitely not because he wanted an extra eighty grand a year. It was pocket change for him.

His house was wedged in between two celebrity mansions. The kind of place that buses visit on tours. The cabbie gave a skeptical look at the elaborate gate guarded by stone lions with uplifted paws and said, "This right?"

"This is right," I said, and I gave him a sweaty wad of cash.

He was gone before I'd gotten all the way to the intercom.

I buzzed. The speaker crackled on, and I said, "It's me, it's Cèsar Hawke."

The gate swung open immediately. Fritz's front lawn was bigger than most public parks. It was early in the morning and gardeners were working on maintaining his flowerbeds. The staff didn't even glance at me as I headed for the front door.

A man emerged from the house, half-dressed for work in charcoal gray slacks. He was a suave motherfucker with his blond hair slicked back, a tie hanging around his neck, and a watch that probably cost more than Domingo's house. I'd always thought he looked kind of like James Bond.

"Cèsar! Thank God!" Was I imagining things, or

did Fritz look relieved to see me?

I lifted my hands in a gesture of surrender. "I'm not here to fight. I'm turning myself in."

"Turning yourself in?" Fritz frowned deeply. "Aren't you going to try to defend yourself?"

"No. I'm just…turning myself in."

"Well," he said. "You surprise me."

I'd surprised myself, too. "I've had a bad week, man."

He obviously already knew that. He swept a hand toward the front door. "Let's go inside. You look like you could use a drink."

Fritz had servants. One of them brought me a snifter of brandy. Not my usual breakfast, but considering I was about to go somewhere that I'd never have a drink like this again, it seemed like a final act of generosity from my boss. Even so, I didn't want to drink it. I never wanted to drink alcohol again. I cupped the snifter between my hands and warmed it with my body heat as Fritz hiked up the legs of his trousers and settled on the chaise across from me.

He looked like he was going to speak. I didn't let him.

"I've been doing some investigating in my… time off. Trying to figure shit out. Get my head on straight. You've probably heard some of it from Eduardo and Joey."

Fritz's eyes sparked with interest. "Agents Costa and Dawes? What about them?"

"They didn't tell you that they found me?" I

asked.

"They haven't been back to work in days."

Well, *that* was interesting. "They caught me at an RV park, dragged me out to the desert, and tried to execute me." Fritz's jaw dropped open. I quickly added, "I left them alive. All I did was tie them up." I didn't mention Isobel. If the OPA didn't know how to find her, I wasn't going to help them.

"I believe you," Fritz said. "I know you wouldn't lie about that." He raked a hand through this hair. "That's not good, Cèsar. Costa and Dawes are with the Union, and as you know, there's somewhat of a...veil of secrecy between our department and theirs. I'll have to go through official channels to get authority to investigate them."

"But you *will* investigate them?"

"I'll investigate," he said.

Relief warmed me. At least something good had come out of this. The only good thing, maybe, but at least it was *something*.

Fritz leaned his elbows on his knees, staring at me intently. "Now do you want to talk about what's happened with Erin Karwell?"

I stared into the brandy. The pattern of the marble floor was distorted through the curved side. "Not really."

"I wish you had come to me when you left the police station."

"Would have made your job easier, huh?" I asked.

He looked surprised. "I might have been able to help you."

"I don't think there's any helping me now." It wasn't about me anyway. Even if he could have waved his hand and made the problem disappear, it wouldn't have fixed anything for Erin.

"You're a good agent, Cèsar. I don't have many good agents under me—and fewer that I can trust. I'd hate to lose you."

Even though I'd killed a woman? "I've always appreciated my job," I said cautiously. "But you didn't send anyone to pick me up from the 77th Street station. I figured you'd written me off."

He shrugged. "The paperwork takes time. You never would have gone to trial."

I didn't know what to say about that. I opened my mouth then shut it.

A man wearing a black suit and tie stepped into the doorway. He caught Fritz's eye. My boss stood.

"Finish your drink," he said. "I have a phone conference I can't miss."

What was more important than a fugitive agent showing up at his door?

As if he could read my mind, Fritz said, "There's been new evidence in your case. They're debriefing me on it now." He gave me a sideways smile. "With this new development, I'm sure the meeting won't last long."

I didn't see anything amusing about it. My fingers tightened on the snifter hard enough that the pads went white.

Fritz followed his security guard or assistant or whatever into the kitchen. I could see through the doorway that Fritz's kitchen was as nice as the rest of his house. Marble countertops, big island thing, cast iron cookware hanging from the rack. There was a freaking waterfall on the back wall.

I wasn't sure how long it would be until the Union came to take me away, but I felt antsy, like I was going to get jumped at any moment. I paced the room, set the brandy on his antique bureau, checked my reflection in the mirror. The week had aged me. I was scruffy and sunburned and dirty.

I scrubbed my jaw and stared at the face of the man who had killed Erin Karwell. That guy deserved everything he was gonna get.

My hip buzzed.

I just about jumped out of my skin at the sensation. Patted my pockets. Felt something hard on the right side.

Domingo's cell phone. I forgot that I'd been carrying it.

I glanced up at the kitchen. Fritz was still talking with his assistant, outlined in gold by the light through the window. They weren't watching me. They didn't notice when I stepped into the hall and answered the cell phone.

"You have to come back, Cèsar."

Took me a second to recognize Isobel's voice. She sounded like she was panicking. "Wait, what? Are you okay? What's wrong?"

"It's Agent Takeuchi—she did it, she was there—"

"Slow down, Izzy. What about Suzy? Where was she?"

"I grabbed some of Erin Karwell's cremains before we ran. I'm sorry, I know it's gross. But I used it to raise her again."

"Why would you—"

"Cèsar, you're as dangerous as a teddy bear. Erin never said that you killed her specifically, did she? I had to know." Isobel plowed on without waiting for me to speak. The reception was bad—her voice crackled, faded, then came back. "—was there that night. At your apartment."

What she was trying to tell me started to sink in.

"Suzy was there?"

"She was fucking *there*, Cèsar," Isobel said. She didn't seem to have heard me. I was losing her. "Erin saw her."

It was impossible. No way Suzy would have been hiding that from me, not without a good reason. It didn't mean she was a killer—it didn't mean *anything*.

"Wait, there's someone—" Isobel began.

The sound crackled, fuzzed, and cut off abruptly.

The call had died.

CHAPTER TWENTY-THREE

FRITZ'S FRONT GATE WAS closed. It was tall. And there were two black SUVs parked on the other side. The Union had arrived to arrest me, take me to a detention center, make me vanish.

They were going to be disappointed.

I veered off the path, hurtling through the gardens. "Sorry!" I shouted to a gardener as I pulverized his begonias.

There was a tree planted near the wall. It had been trimmed to keep the branches from hanging over the opposite side, but it was easy to climb from the gardens. Domingo and I had climbed a thousand trees to sneak out and party on the weekends, and my muscle memory hadn't faded. I was over the wall in seconds.

I jumped over the side. Landed hard on my knees. Got up to run.

Hands grabbed my jacket from behind. I swung a right hook as I turned.

It was only Suzy's lightning-fast reaction time that saved her from getting a face full of fist. She grabbed my wrist and twisted it behind my back. I felt my elbow pop.

"Suzy!"

She forced me to the ground with her grip on my arm. "Shut the fuck up, Cèsar," she hissed under her breath. "They're on the other side of that wall."

Once she was sure I was quiet, she released me and leaned around the corner to look at the SUVs. Her hand rested on her hip where a holster should have been. For the first time, I wondered why she hadn't been carrying her sidearm. I hadn't seen her with it in days.

"What are you doing here?" I asked.

"Looking for you." She showed me a crystal filled with a faint turquoise glow. "Tracking spell. I used the clothes you left at my house as a focus."

"Why? Because you want to tell me the truth about what happened the night Erin died?"

The blood drained out of her face. "Cèsar—"

"So it's true."

Her lips pressed into a thin frown. "Stonecrow?"

I nodded.

She pushed her hair out of her face, closed her eyes, seemed to think silently for a moment. When her eyes opened again, she looked resigned. "You were drunk off your ass, Hawke. You'd been arguing with the waitress outside. When I saw you leave with her, I followed to save you from a drunken one night stand."

"And then?" I pressed.

"I confronted the two of you in the parking lot outside your place. I told Erin to go home and offered to pay for a cab." She glanced at me. Then back down. Couldn't meet my eyes. "You had your tongue halfway down her throat, but you found the oxygen to tell me to fuck off."

"So you shot her?"

Suzy's eyes widened. "What? No. I fucked off, like you told me to. I went home."

"You knew what I'd done this whole time," I said.

"Of course I did. I'm not stupid, Cèsar. Everyone knows what you did. Everyone fucking saw you leave The Pit with Erin Karwell."

"If you were so intent on hiding the truth from me, then why did you take Isobel and me to the morgue?"

"I didn't think Stonecrow would actually be able to talk to the dead. I read her files. I was convinced she was bullshitting you, bullshitting everyone, and that she'd just make something up that made you happy. I didn't think she'd tell you that you actually…" She stopped talking. Shut her mouth.

My head was swimming. I felt sick.

I didn't realize I'd sunk into a crouch until her hand dropped onto my shoulder.

"They're going to arrest you, Cèsar, and who knows what comes after that? We need to get out of here."

This time, when she grabbed me, I let her. She ran toward the street behind the house. I followed her.

A black SUV stopped at the end of the alley.

She skidded to a stop. Planted both hands in

my chest, pushed me the other way.

But when I turned, there was a black SUV there, too. We'd been caught on both sides. Now men were jumping out wearing tactical gear, shouting for us to freeze, drop our guns, put our hands in the air. Suzy was swearing again.

"I'll talk us out of this," she said.

I lifted my hands to my shoulders. My heart wasn't even beating fast now. I wasn't scared of facing what was to come—what I deserved to deal with.

The men stepped into the alley and circled us. Six of them, all carrying M16s and wearing ballistic helmets. Their flak jackets had bold white letters on the chest: "UKA." It was a full unit of Union kopides—and they weren't messing around.

But when Suzy stepped away from me, saying, "He's not a threat," the guns aimed at her.

Not me. Suzy.

"Cèsar!" It was Fritz. He stood just outside the ring of armed men. His shirt was buttoned with a perfect double Windsor at his throat. "Approach me slowly," he said, holding out a hand.

He was talking to *me*.

I blinked at him. "What?"

"Suzume Takeuchi, you're under arrest for the murder of Erin Karwell," said one of the Union men.

"This was the subject of the conference call, Cèsar. They identified the partial fingerprints on the Glock we found in your apartment," Fritz said, voice shockingly level. "The gun belongs to Agent Takeuchi."

"Suzy?" I asked.

Suzy was shaking her head, her expression slowly melting into horror. "It was stolen from my house. My broken windows—they took the Glock—"

A man whipped the butt of his M16 into the back of her head. She cried out, but stayed on her feet and tried to escape. Then there were three men on her, forcing her to the ground facedown. Her arms were twisted behind her back. They cuffed her.

Fritz approached with a black bag in hand. He looked grim.

"I'm sorry, Cèsar," he said. "I know you were close friends."

Were—past tense. Like Suzy was already gone.

And then he pulled the bag over her head and cinched it.

CHAPTER TWENTY-FOUR

EVERYTHING WAS A BLUR after that.

I was debriefed in an SUV as they took me home. Fritz rode along in back with me, fielding multiple phone calls, occasionally barking orders over a Bluetooth headset. He told me that I was totally innocent. He told me that my arrest record with the LAPD had already been wiped.

I asked him what would happen to Suzy.

He said, "She'll be detained."

Fritz had no offers of leniency for Suzy, no laments about what a trustworthy agent she was and how much he would miss her. Just a stony glare and a comforting pat on my back.

"I don't think Suzy's guilty," I said.

How could I explain that Erin's ghost had told me I was the murderer? The dead couldn't lie. Suzy *couldn't* be guilty. But I couldn't say any of that without giving Isobel away, and it wouldn't explain how Suzy's Glock had killed the waitress.

"Take the afternoon to relax," Fritz said, handing a security badge to the Magical Violations building to me. It had my picture on it and no other information. "I look forward to seeing you at the office tomorrow."

We'd arrived at my apartment complex.

I stepped out. The SUVs left.

And then I was alone.

My home was totally clean now. Erin's blood had been scrubbed out of the carpet, and the smell of cleaning fluid lingered in the air. My DVDs were intact. Someone had removed my broken appliances. All my potions and poultices were gone. Aside from that, it looked normal.

It didn't feel like I belonged there.

And I definitely didn't want to go anywhere near my bathroom.

Instead, I grabbed Domingo's Charger from the parking lot near Helltown and went for a drive.

Isobel's RV wasn't where she had left it. All I found was a drying stain where her septic system had been drained and tire tracks.

She was gone.

I sat behind the wheel of the Charger for a good twenty minutes, thinking back on our last phone call, the way it had cut off. She'd probably been using a cheap burner phone, since a nomad without a job could hardly get a contract with a major carrier. No surprise that there'd been bad reception. The fact that she was gone probably didn't mean she was in trouble—just that she'd moved on the way she always had. Off to find another source of income.

Not a big deal. That was her *modus operandi*.

Always on the move. Shouldn't take it personally.

But I did.

Hey, she'd been the one to kiss me, even when she thought I'd killed Erin. Couldn't blame me for thinking she might be interested in seeing me again now that I was, apparently, an innocent man.

Whatever.

Fritz had told me to take the afternoon off, but I couldn't imagine returning to my apartment. It was still early in the day, not even noon.

I turned on the Charger and drove to my first day of work since Erin Karwell's death.

I had the security badge Fritz had given me, but when I walked up to the monolithic white building of the Magical Violations Department, I didn't really expect it to work. It felt like everyone was staring at me as I walked through the OPA campus, accusing me of murder with their glares—or worse, of betraying Suzy.

No way they'd let me in. Not after the sins I'd committed.

But the card reader flashed green when I waved the badge over it. The door unlocked. I stepped inside, and nobody stopped me.

My desk was in cubeville on the third floor. The exterior walls were giant windows looking out over the campus. Within those windows, everything was surrounded by boring gray half walls. No privacy for the witches working in Magical Violations.

Conversations stopped and heads turned as I headed for my desk by the north windows.

I sat down at my desk to find that all of my belongings had been cleared from the surface—not just mine, but Suzy's, too. Every last scrap of it. Her cup of pens. Her computer monitor. The pink and yellow sticky notes we had been using to leave obscene jokes for each other. The three little ceramic cats she used to keep next to the stapler.

It looked so empty.

Aniruddha stopped by, tapping a knuckle on my desk. "Hey, Hawke. You've probably noticed something's missing."

My eyes were drawn to Suzy's chair, pushed into the corner with nobody sitting in it.

"A few things are missing, yeah," I said.

"All of your personal effects and work computer were taken down to processing," Aniruddha said. "Friederling has requested that everything be returned to you as soon as possible. Luckily your effects didn't get taken to the warehouse yet, but it's still going to take a couple hours to find everything. You'll be back to normal by tomorrow morning."

Normal. Right.

"Thanks, man," I said.

He glanced at the empty chair, too. "Never would have believed it. Didn't believe it when they said it was you, either."

"Thanks," I said again because I didn't know what else to say.

"I don't think you'll be able to get any work done until your computer is back. You should go for a walk. Get something to eat. Go home." He shrugged. "Up to you."

And then Aniruddha left, checking his clipboard for the next item on his to-do list.

Maybe that wasn't a bad idea, going for a walk. But I wasn't hungry. I was still jazzed from all the energy potions I'd been mainlining for the last few days and my stomach had cramped into one hard knot.

I headed down to processing instead. It was the office where they tagged and organized evidence before filing it away in a warehouse for the rest of eternity.

I'd only ever seen one woman working the desk there. Ivy was older than dirt but sharper than shale. She worked in a cinder block room in the basement of the OPA office. Its high windows were barred. There were three aisles of tables with evidence waiting to be filed. Everything was tagged with slips of pink, yellow, blue, and green paper.

I'm sure it seemed organized to Ivy, but it looked like insanity to me.

She snapped her fingers when she saw me come through the door and said, "Case File 4457-A. I'm on top of it."

"Thanks, Ivy," I said.

Ivy went searching for my case file number, shuffling between the tables, pushing her glasses up the bridge of her nose, muttering to herself.

A CD on the table next to me caught my eye. It was sitting in the sunlight label-down and casting a rainbow on the wall. It was tagged with green paper.

"What's green mean?" I asked.

Ivy didn't even look at me. "Evidence seized by the Union."

"It gets mixed up in here too?"

"Oh yes. That's a good way of putting it. 'Mixed up.' I swear to you, if they would just take care to label things *before* sending them to me..." Ivy sniffed delicately. "The Union is the worst about it, too. I just had two boxes of evidence from Costa and Dawes brought to me, and it's like they were deliberately attempting to obfuscate their evidence! It'll take days for me to review and sort through it all. *Days.*"

The disc had been taken from Eduardo and Joey? While Ivy was still distracted, I flipped the disc over. It had been printed with a time and date—the day before Erin's murder. And Ivy was right about obfuscation. Someone had blacked out the case number with marker.

I grabbed it. Tucked it into my pocket.

Ivy turned around, setting a box on the table in front of me. It had a pink label. Why did the Union get to be green when Magical Violations was freaking *pink*? "The personal effects taken from your apartment will take longer to return. We need to seize them from the LAPD. Everything you need to do your job should be in here, however."

I took the box from her. I managed a smile. "Thanks."

CHAPTER TWENTY-FIVE

I WENT HOME TO check out the CD in privacy.

It was the first time I'd taken my work-issued laptop back to my apartment. I sat at my kitchen table as the disc drive whirred to life, nursing a tall glass of chocolate-flavored protein powder and almond milk. It wasn't sitting well in my cramping stomach, but I needed the sustenance. Anything but another energy potion.

Before I opened the video program, I checked to make sure the Wi-Fi and Bluetooth were turned off—didn't want the laptop reporting to the OPA that I was reviewing stolen evidence. It might have been paranoid, but whatever. I felt like I had earned some paranoia.

Then I clicked the video. I fully expected it to be surveillance of my apartment, or maybe The Pit.

But the gray picture that appeared on the screen was of Suzy's house.

I felt a wave of shock at the sight of her familiar couches and coffee table. Cat was lying on one of her chairs, kneading a blanket in his paws. The windows were open—Suzy hadn't been burgled yet. Clicking the fast-forward button, I watched Cat sleep at four times normal speed, his furry flank rising and falling rapidly. He got up, licked his ass, went back to sleep on a couch. Night fell outside. Cat chased a fly and then disappeared.

Motion flashed outside Suzy's window, but the video was going too quickly for me to be able to tell what it was. I resumed normal speed. Reversed. Hit play.

A human figure crossed through the shadows outside.

I watched the next five minutes with my breath stuck in my throat. The intruder didn't come through that window. She came in somewhere off screen and walked through the living room with her back to the camera. Fished around under the coffee table, searched Suzy's filing cabinet.

Then the intruder turned as if she could feel the camera looking at her.

I paused the video.

Her face was square and framed with heavy brown hair. Her lips were full. I would know—I'd kissed those lips.

Isobel had broken into Suzy's house.

As the video continued, I watched Isobel break into Suzy's gun safe. She grabbed the Glock. It didn't look like she was comfortable with firearms; she seemed to accidentally eject the magazine and struggled to reinsert it.

But then she turned suddenly, as if responding to a noise that the footage didn't pick up. A man walked into the frame. He had a slender figure, long black hair, studded leather jacket—an incubus?

Isobel's mouth moved silently. She aimed the gun.

He flashed across the screen, moving toward her with superhuman speed.

She fired. The muzzle flashed. Black blood spurted from the back of her assailant's jacket.

And that was all of the footage.

I replayed it to make sure, searched for other files on the disc, but that was it. There had to be more after that—it just wasn't on the CD.

I ejected the disc and checked the date again.

It was the day *before* Erin's murder. Two days before I'd hunted down Isobel.

But there she was, breaking into Suzy's house, caught on footage from a security camera that I was pretty sure didn't belong to Suzy. The OPA had put surveillance in her house. I looked over my shoulder, thinking I'd see a guy in a black suit standing over me, and didn't find anything. I was going to have to search my whole fucking apartment for cameras and microphones before I took another shower.

I didn't put the disc back in. The image of Isobel struggling with a demon was still frozen on the screen even though I'd removed the CD.

The disc had belonged to my case, but been deliberately damaged by Eduardo and Joey. Why? What was it about Isobel's fight with the incubus that they didn't want anyone to know? Or was it the information that exonerated Suzy that they were trying to hide?

Because this definitely exonerated her—and

implicated someone else entirely. Someone I never would have suspected.

Suzy had said that the Glock had been stolen from her house, and here Isobel was, doing the stealing. That Glock had appeared in my living room the night that Erin died.

I slammed the laptop shut and left the apartment.

The evening was growing long by the time I reached Helltown. I parked the Charger in the Walmart lot again before heading under the invisible arch.

This time, I thought to duck rather than getting a femur to the face.

The streets of Helltown were just as busy as the last time I'd been there—maybe even busier. It was getting late. The weaker demons were trying to get inside before night fell, and the stronger demons were preparing for another night of fun. A night that I didn't plan on sticking around to see.

I'd gone in through the entrance closest to the Temple of the Hand of Death, and I sprinted straight there without looking back. I had to move through shadows to reach it. Every time I left direct sunlight, I felt a chill rake down my spine. Felt like eyes on my back. Creatures watching me. Waiting for a chance to feed. Maybe even Silver Needles closing in to try to kill me again.

I didn't plan on giving them a chance.

The front door of the Temple of the Hand of Death hung off its hinges. And Isobel's RV was parked next to the empty gas pumps.

Drawing my Desert Eagle, I threw open the door to her RV and checked inside. There was nothing there but the beaded curtains. No sign of a struggle—but no sign of Isobel's whereabouts either.

I kept the gun aimed at the ground as I moved into the temple. There were no electric lights inside, so the shadows were deep. An oil lamp left smoky smears on the wall and didn't penetrate the darkness all the way back to the altar. But it was enough light for me to see that the teenage priestess was sprawled on the floor in a mess of velvet skirts and blood. What had Isobel called her? Ann?

She stirred as I dropped to her side. She wasn't dead. Thank God.

I holstered the gun. "Are you okay?"

"What do you think?" She pushed her skirts aside to reveal the hilt of a dagger jutting from her fleshy leg. She had been stabbed. My stomach lurched at the sight of it.

She needed medical support. An ambulance. The kind of help that couldn't come into Helltown.

"Are you alone here?" I asked.

"I am now," Ann said. She sat straight up, scanning the ground surrounding her. When her gaze fell on the stone scepter that had fallen a few feet away, she immediately seized it. Hugged it to her chest. "They took Isobel." Still clutching the scepter tightly, the girl yanked the knife out of her thigh.

"Whoa there," I said, standing back with my hands lifted, unsure if I should try to help her. "Be careful. The femoral artery—"

"It didn't hit anything major. Don't worry about it. I'll be fine." She sounded calm, but she was sweating. She glared at me with furious blue eyes. "This is sacred ground. Isobel should have been safe here."

"What happened? Was it an incubus?"

Ann frowned. "No, it was a guy dressed like you." I was dressed for work—so, black suit, white shirt, black tie. OPA standard. Probably Eduardo.

"Do you know where he took her, Ann?"

"He said something about a pit when he dragged her out of here," Ann said. "That's all I know."

"Wait. *A* pit, or *The* Pit?"

"Dunno." She wiped her blood off the dagger with her forefinger, then rubbed it on the shaft of the scepter. I couldn't help but recoil. The blood was…vanishing. Like the scepter was drinking it up. Any urge I'd had to protect this girl was suddenly gone. Isobel was right. Ann didn't need to be saved by anyone—definitely not my responsibility.

"Do you need me to take you to a hospital?" I asked, even though I already knew the answer.

"We'll be fine," Ann said.

We? Hadn't she said that she was alone? I backed away from her, eyeing the darkening streets outside the shattered windows. I needed to get out before the Needles realized I was there—and before the worse demons came out to play.

I left Ann alone in the darkness.

CHAPTER TWENTY-SIX

THE OLIVE PIT SHOULD have been open at six o'clock in the evening, but its neon sign was turned off and the windows were dark. I sat across the street in the Charger for a good long minute, arguing silently with myself over how I should approach it: Go in alone, or call for backup?

Procedure said that I should call for help. We were expected to work with a certain level of autonomy—probably more than the real FBI were—but when it came to situations potentially involving firearms, we were supposed to get Union support. If a witch cast a spell at me, I could cancel it out with my own magic, but magic didn't do much against bullets. And Eduardo would definitely be armed.

But I didn't know whom to call anymore. Suzy had been arrested for a murder she couldn't have committed by the company we worked for. Eduardo and Joey were definitely bad guys. And Fritz—who knew about Fritz? He had contributed to Suzy's arrest, too.

I sent a text message to one of the only phone

numbers I had memorized then got out of the car.

The windows were unlit, but the curtains were open, so I peered inside. There was a light on in the kitchen, but everything else was turned off.

Silhouettes moved in front of the illuminated doorway. I counted them.

Five distinct men. I could tell them apart by their heights and clothing. And those were just the ones I could see.

I sat against the side of the building as I considered my odds, hiding out of sight from the men inside. Handling a single witch was easy. That was what I did best. Stalking them, figuring out their patterns, slipping a sleeping potion into their coffee. No confrontation necessary.

But five guys—I didn't know where to begin.

"You really think this is time for a drink?"

I whirled. Domingo stood in the mouth of the alley. He wore another comfortable sweatsuit and carried a brown paper bag.

"You got here fast," I said.

"I saw on the news that Agent Takeuchi is going to trial for the waitress's murder, so I figured you were declared innocent. I was already on my way to bring you dinner at your apartment. Up for celebratory junk food?" He tipped the bag and the smell of cheeseburgers wafted through the air.

I hadn't been hungry until that moment. I snagged his sleeve, pulled him down to the ground with me, tore into the bag. "We've got a problem," I said around a mouthful of burger. "There are at least five men inside this building and they're holding Isobel captive."

Domingo tensed. "So you texted *me*?"

"I can't handle it alone."

"Call in backup! You're with the FBI!"

I swallowed down one of the burgers. "Actually, I'm not. I work for a secret government department called the Office of Preternatural Affairs. We handle witches gone bad and demons and stuff. I don't know if I can trust anyone with the OPA now. All I know is I can trust *you*."

He made the time out symbol with his hands. "You shitting me?"

"What? Abuelita's a witch, we're witches. Are demons that weird?"

"No, I knew about demons. I mean this Office of Whatever the Fuck."

"You knew about demons?"

"Do you think you're the only one Ofelia talks to? Yes, I know about demons. But I thought that secret government stuff was some tinfoil hat bullshit."

"Oh yeah, newsflash. Secret government agencies exist. I work for one." I shrugged. "I'm not supposed to tell anyone, but I figure this is better than getting killed. So—ideas?"

Domingo sat back against the wall, staring up at the sliver of sky we could see between the two buildings. Clouds were moving in again. Smelled like rain. He was probably thinking about what I'd told him, but I knew it wouldn't take him long to wrap his brain around it. My brother was tough as fuck.

"Isobel," he said after a minute. "The woman you were telling me about."

"Yeah. The woman."

"She worth saving?"

Was she? She'd stolen Suzy's Glock and gotten my friend detained. But she'd also been taken by Eduardo or Joey. If she'd framed Suzy, then she needed to come to justice—and not the vigilante kind.

The thought of turning Isobel over to the OPA didn't sit well, either.

Cross that bridge once I come to it.

"She's worth it," I said.

Domingo grabbed the last burger out of the bag and scarfed it down. Once he was done, he wiped his hands off on his sweats and stood up. "'Kay. I've got an idea."

Domingo had everything he needed in the trunk of his car—his "mobile command center," he joked. He tossed me a big black can of salt and a skein of yarn and told me to help him circle the building. He'd take the north and east sides; I'd take the west and south.

"Don't let anyone see you," I warned him.

Domingo flashed a dazzling smile. "Me?"

This was the guy that had once stolen a dozen MacBook Pro laptops from an Apple Store while it was open—and escaped without getting caught. Casting a circle of power around a bar filled with demons unseen was nothing compared to his battle with the Geniuses.

I still moved to cast my half of the circle as fast as I could. I kept low, crouched under the windows, and unspooled the yarn as fast as possible. Then I joined up with Domingo in the back alley. He clapped his hands to close the circle, and the shock of magic was strong enough to make me sneeze twice.

"Shut up," he said, clapping a hand over my mouth. I sneezed on him. "Sick, dude."

I scrubbed my face clean. "What now?"

"Sleeping spell," Domingo said. "The Cèsar Hawke Special. I got all the herbs you recommended—including passionflower—so all we have to do is amplify and project it." He tossed a gemstone to me. An emerald the size of my thumbnail. "I'll get the chants going over here. Put this on the western point of the circle. Once the spell activates, take the emerald and head inside with it—everyone'll be unconscious."

I rolled the gem over in my fingers. "Everyone?"

"Everyone but the guy holding the emerald."

That'd make getting Isobel out tricky. But hey, it also meant skipping a fight and getting my ass kicked. I'd take it.

"What are you doing driving around with the supplies for sleeping spells?" I asked.

"I'd been planning to take it around to test it on friends. Well, covenmates. Help me tweak it a little, you know?" He planted his hands on his hips, giving the circle's circumference a hard look. "This should probably work."

"Probably? I'm feeling real confident in your skills right now."

He grinned. "Go save the woman, Cèsar."

CHAPTER TWENTY-SEVEN

THE MAGIC WAS ALREADY building by the time I reached the front of the building. I was fighting so hard against the urge to sneeze that my eyes were streaming, blurring the street around me. But even though my vision was shot, I could see that one of The Pit's windows was suddenly open.

All of the windows had been closed when I'd checked the building out earlier.

I dropped into a crouch, hiding below the windowsill. I could hear footsteps on the other side of the wall. Whoever had opened the window was still nearby.

On all fours, I crawled to the edge of the circle and set the emerald on the western point. It sparked with blue light.

Domingo's magic surged, sudden and powerful. The sneeze caught me off-guard. My face pretty much exploded—and the sound echoed.

Shit.

The front door unlocked behind me.

I was standing by the time it swung open, but I didn't draw my gun in time. Eduardo Costa stared at me from the other side. He looked as surprised to see me as I was to see him. He wasn't wearing a jacket, so I could see that he had a shoulder rig with a holster under each arm.

"Cèsar," he hissed.

I socked him in the jaw.

Eduardo didn't even flinch.

He tackled me to the ground and we hit the pavement hard. He was heavy on top of me, knee digging into my chest, compressing my lungs. But my difficulties breathing were the least of my problems. If he moved two inches to the right, he would break Domingo's circle of power. Scuffing that line of salt would kill the spell instantly.

Had to get him back inside the building.

Blows rained down on me fast and hard. Couldn't even tell where Eduardo was hitting. Everything from the shoulders up hurt like fireworks detonating in my bones. I blocked my face, absorbing the contact with my forearms.

He paused to draw a gun.

It only took a second—but it was long enough. I sat up. Slammed my head into his face. Missed his nose, but sent him reeling.

The emerald flared just a few inches away from my head as Domingo's magic snapped into place. The burst of energy meant that anyone inside the building should have gone unconscious.

Too bad Eduardo was outside.

I grabbed the emerald and held it in my fist as I swung. I knocked Eduardo's arm aside at the same instant that he fired. The bullet went wide, smacked into the stucco exterior of The Pit. The sound was loud enough that my aching skull began to ring like a bell.

He turned to aim again. I dived, shoving him through the doorway.

We both crossed the threshold.

The instant his foot touched the ground, his eyes went blank. He rag-dolled on the ground. Caught a table on the way down. It collapsed under his weight, cracking and crashing underneath him.

I caught my breath, prepared to pass out with him.

But I was awake. The emerald was warm in my hand.

"Domingo, you genius bastard," I whispered.

I held still for a moment, listening for the sound of others on the approach. Anyone who was awake should have heard the gunfire and come running, but my brother's spell seemed to have worked. Everything was silent inside The Pit.

Kneeling beside Eduardo's body, I patted him down for weapons. All I found were the two guns under his arms. They were smaller than mine— each one a Beretta 9mm, both probably Union-issued. That was a pretty standard model of gun for police and military. I still had my Desert Eagle, but I took one of pistols anyway. Having twelve extra bullets couldn't hurt.

I checked the safety, then tucked Eduardo's gun in the back of my belt and went looking for Isobel.

There were more bodies near the kitchen. I had expected to find Joey nearby, but was shocked to see that these men weren't OPA employees at all—

they were slender men with black hair and leather jackets. I thumbed back an eyelid on one of them. His irises were demon-black.

What was Eduardo doing hanging out with incubi?

And they weren't just any incubi. The guy I was looking at was wearing a leather jacket pinned shut with silver needles. The wickedly sharp edges were stained brown.

These were the same fuckers who had hurt Ofelia and attacked me in Helltown.

And they had Isobel.

A storm of righteous fury and protectiveness surged in my chest. It was too easy to imagine Isobel looking like Ofelia had when I found her at the beach house. All the punctures in her ears, her nose, her lips, the back of her neck.

Not again.

I followed the beam of light through the kitchen door. That was where I found Thandy—the manager that I'd interviewed right after Erin died. She didn't look injured, and she had a pulse. She'd be fine once Domingo lifted his spell. That accounted for four of the people I had seen in the kitchens. There was at least one other around here somewhere.

A door next to the walk-in freezer was opened. It led to basement stairs.

I headed down.

The basement was cold and dry, with a dirt floor and brick walls. They had several floor-to-ceiling racks of wine bottles, a few kegs stacked in the corner, and some other assorted liquor on the shelves. Guess it was what I would have expected to find underneath a bar.

The chair with a woman tied to it, though—I was pretty sure that wasn't normal for a bar.

I rounded the steel chair to find that Isobel's ankles and wrists had been tied to it. Her head drooped low, chin touching her chest. I gently pushed her head back and was relieved to see that she hadn't been tortured yet—not with needles, anyway. She had a black eye. Her bottom lip was split open in two places. Blood had dried on her chin.

"Jesus, Izzy," I muttered.

I holstered my gun and worked at the knot on her right wrist, picking at it with my stubby fingernails. It had been tied tightly by an expert. It wasn't loosening. I had to resort to biting at it to get the thing undone. *Thank God everyone else is unconscious.* I must have looked like an insane pit bull gnawing on her ropes.

Luckily, the other knots came more easily. I was working on her left ankle when I felt Domingo's spell fail.

A frisson of energy settled over me, like I'd stepped under one of those grocery store produce misters. Breathing became easier immediately as my nose stopped itching.

The magic was gone. The circle had broken.

And I was still in the basement of The Pit.

"Step back. Hands in the air."

I settled back on my heels, mind racing through all of my favorite swear words, both real and invented for the situation. "You woke up fast," I said, looking over my shoulder to see Eduardo on the stairs. He still had one gun. Guess I should have taken both of those from him.

He scrubbed a hand over his eyes. Took another two steps into the basement.

"I should be thanking you," Eduardo said. "I thought that Erin was going to get the bounty. But you fixed that problem for me, didn't you? Sounds like I'll be the one to enjoy the payday now."

Wait. Erin was going to get the bounty? What bounty?

Isobel was stirring behind me. Had to get her out of there—first priority. Questions could come later.

The door opened again.

"Don't shoot him. He's *mine*."

My heart stopped beating at the sight of the second man that had stepped onto the stairs. His hair was choppily short and inky-black. His skin was pale, his eyes endless pits of darkness. And there was a tattoo encircling his neck—feathered wings that touched his chin with the tips.

It was the incubus that had tortured Ofelia.

My hatred was immediate, but brief. The incubus had brought raw sexual energy with him. His thrall crashed into me. Sucked my breath away.

All I could think of was naked bodies. Sweaty skin. Lips and fingers.

"Hey, I caught him first, Gregor," Eduardo protested.

Gregor. The incubus was named Gregor.

"And I told you not to shoot him," the demon said, cracking his knuckles. I stared at his fingers and thought about them wrapped around my hardening shaft. I couldn't help it—couldn't clear the image from my mind, no matter how hard I fought it.

I'd been able to resist the Needles in Helltown, but this guy was a thousand times more powerful than that. I was the tree bowed under the weight of the hurricane. I was nothing.

I *needed* him.

Eduardo was still talking, but I barely heard him. "If you think this means you don't have to pay me the bounty—"

"I don't," Gregor said.

Fuck it, kill him. Kill him now before the thrall's too much.

I moved in slow motion. Stood, turned, drawing my Desert Eagle.

My hands were clumsy on the metal. Didn't want to be wrapped around a gun, didn't want my finger curved around the trigger. My dick was hardening, straining against my fly. I wanted my clothes off. I wanted Gregor. I *knew* it was thrall, and it didn't matter.

I aimed the gun at Gregor's head but couldn't pull the trigger. His black eyes were sucking me in. He extended a hand toward me and the tension between us grew to a fever pitch until I couldn't tell that Eduardo was still in the room. Hell, even Isobel didn't matter anymore—the woman I'd broken into The Pit to save. It was just the incubus and me.

The demon that had tortured my sister.

Shoot him. Now.

The Desert Eagle slipped out of my hand. Hit the ground.

My trigger finger tensed after the gun was already gone. Seconds too late. The only explosion I heard was my will self-destructing.

I tried to draw Eduardo's Beretta, but then the incubus was on top of me, slamming me into the wall, punching me across the jaw. It felt good. Like pleasure erupting down my spine. I wanted him to do it again. I wanted him to rip my throat out and drink the blood and ride me down into darkness. I'd bleed for him, drain every fluid dry if Gregor asked.

Ofelia had turned this down for a week. A *week*.

Thirty seconds of it and I was ready to give in.

Gregor punched me again. "I've been waiting years," he growled, punctuating each word with another strike. "You. Almost. Killed. Me."

"More," I said. The word came out unbidden. My balls were getting tight, on the verge of erupting. My hands were empty—I'd dropped the Beretta, too.

This is thrall, you have to shake it, you have to get free...

Knuckles met the bridge of my nose. Felt something snap. Tasted blood.

It was good. So damn good.

"You ruined my life!" Gregor said. "You made me look impotent in front of the Needles when you took that bitch away. And I had to cut a fucking deal with the Union to get out of the detention center. Do you know what that did to my pride?"

Why was he so angry with me? I just wanted to

please him—whatever it would take for him to keep pleasing *me*.

"I thought I'd settle for your head," he said, grabbing my shirt in both hands, jerking my face close to his. "But this is better than that. I'm *much* happier killing you myself."

"More," I whispered again.

"I'll give you more, you motherfucker."

Gregor threw me.

I was flying.

The room hurtled past me. My back hit something hard, something that didn't feel like liquid sex. Heard glass shatter. I collapsed to the dirt and wine bottles rained around me.

The shelf hit me a second later.

That one hurt.

The pain was almost enough to snap me out of the incubus's thrall. I remembered fighting him on the beach after saving Ofelia. I remembered slamming him into the rocks, cracking his head open, watching the blood gush over the sand.

Incubi were weak. Any injury could make them bleed to death.

Easy.

But I had to hurt him to exploit that—I had to *want* to hurt him.

Eduardo was shivering as he fought against Gregor's thrall. Kopides were less susceptible to demon attack. It still must have hurt like hell. "If you kill Agent Hawke—if you don't pay me that bounty—we're going to have a major problem, Gregor."

The incubus's laugh was like a deep tiger

growl. "I don't think so, Costa. It sure doesn't look like you're the one killing him." A boot slammed into my temple. My vision blurred. I bucked against the ground, pleasure hardening my abs.

"I'll send you back to the detention center," Eduardo said.

Gregor grinned. "You'll have to tell them how I got out in the first place."

He kicked me again and I groaned.

I was screwed. Isobel was screwed. She needed me, and here I was, about to shoot my load on the ground while an incubus fucking beat me to death.

Through the haze, I focused on Isobel.

She must have been hit by the incubus's thrall too, even though Gregor was focusing most of his power on me. She was breathing hard, cheeks flushed, tongue darting out to wet her lips. But she'd broken free of the chair. Apparently, her embarrassing experience in Helltown had taught her how to momentarily shake off incubus thrall—and a moment was all she needed.

Isobel extended her hands over the dirt floor. Her eyes were rolled into the back of her skull. She trembled all over, from her bottom lip to the tips of her fingers.

Magic surged hard, like a fist that squeezed my lungs shut. I couldn't sneeze. I couldn't *breathe*.

Silvery mist rose from the ground around her. Ten different locations around the room—no, more than that. There were graves all over the place. Under the rubble of the wine rack. Under Isobel's chair. Along the walls.

The Needles had been burying victims under

The Pit.

And now Isobel was calling them.

Holy hell.

Gregor stopped kicking me and focused on the silver figures that had just appeared around us. They were all bald and eyeless and glowing, and they surrounded Gregor and Eduardo.

"Get them," Isobel said. The lips of every spirit she had raised moved with hers. She spoke in many voices, deep and tremulous and echoing.

The spirits rushed.

The incubus's thrall couldn't do anything to the dead. He roared as they fell on him, beating his fists at empty air, unable to touch them. The weight of his demon powers lifted from me fractionally, and I searched wildly for the guns I had dropped.

My Desert Eagle was only a few feet away.

I struggled onto my knees, shoving the toppled shelves off of me. I was glad it actually hurt. It helped clear my head, shoving all the scraps of Gregor's thrall out of the corners of my skull.

Gunfire exploded through the room. Eduardo was shooting. It did nothing to the spirits piling on top of him, tearing at him with translucent hands.

Once a spirit stepped onto me, I realized why he was screaming. A foot plunged into my chest. Icy shock froze my heart.

The room went black, and I spiraled toward death.

"Cèsar!"

Isobel's voice broke through the darkness. I heard something skitter, felt metal touch my fingertips. Eduardo's Beretta. She'd kicked it to me.

I grabbed it and got onto my knees.

The spirit slipped out of my body, leaving me gasping.

Eduardo and the incubi had retreated toward the stairs, where the other incubi from upstairs had joined them. Four guys altogether. The spirits wouldn't be able to hold them off for long.

Isobel had given us a distraction, but that was it. Just a fleeting moment to break free of Gregor's thrall. And I could tell Isobel was going to lose control if we didn't get out of there fast. She was shaking hard enough that it looked like she'd break apart.

"Isobel!" I reached for her through silver mist. She didn't seem to see me.

The basement windows shattered. Black figures flew into the room and dropped onto the ground.

Men aimed their guns at us, shouting to each other, shouting at everyone. "Drop your weapons! Hands in the air!"

I caught a flash of black and white Union equipment out of the corner of my eye. Didn't dare look too close, but I knew it was the cavalry. I dropped the gun, put my hands behind my head, stood stock-still.

Eduardo fired.

At least, I think he fired first. All the shouts turned to the chatter of automatic gunfire too quickly for me to tell.

Instinct carried me through the silvery spirits that Isobel had summoned, launching myself toward her with hands outstretched. Ice clutched my heart. But I wrapped my arms around her, slamming both of us to the ground as gunfire exploded overhead. Bullets whizzed over us.

Her eyes cleared the second we hit the ground. "Cèsar?"

The ghosts vanished.

Eduardo struck the earth next to me. Unlike Isobel, his face was blank. Blood cascaded out of his mouth. And then Gregor landed behind them.

Both of them had been shot in the chest. Just like Erin Karwell.

CHAPTER TWENTY-EIGHT

IT SEEMED LIKE THE fight ended real fast after that. The incubi went down fast, and there wasn't enough time for them to summon up a nasty thrall to save their asses. Demons hit the ground, one after another—boom, boom, boom.

The Pit was secure. Isobel and I were safe.

As soon as everything was dead, the Union guys stepped aside to let the OPA agents step in. They weren't from my department, Magical Violations. Considering that we were dealing with incubi, they'd probably come from the Infernal Relations Department—IRD—so I didn't know their names. I'd seen them in the cafeteria at work, though. The faces were familiar.

And then there was another familiar face. Fritz kicked an incubus body down the stairs as he stormed into the basement.

"Cèsar," he said when he saw me. Then his gaze fell on Isobel and his eyes lit up. "Belle!"

Fritz hauled Isobel to her feet and kissed her.

I'd like to say that was less shocking than coming up against the Needles at The Pit, but it wasn't. Surprise squirmed right through my adrenaline haze. All I could do was stare at my boss and the necrocognitive he'd ordered me to find. A necrocognitive that he knew *really* well, apparently.

"Are you hurt?" he asked, cupping her face in both hands.

She pushed him away. Her face was bright red under the bruises. "Don't do that."

"They beat you, didn't they?"

"Cèsar kept them from doing worse," Isobel said.

Fritz barely glanced at me. "Well done, Hawke." *Hawke*? Since when did we stop being on a first-name basis? "Belle, we need an EMT to look at you. Come with me."

He dragged her away.

Isobel caught my eye and mouthed, *Just a second*.

I stared after her for a good two minutes, trying to figure out what the fuck had just happened.

Everything from the last week seemed disjointed, like a puzzle that didn't quite fit together. I understood that Gregor had put a bounty on my head. I also understood that Eduardo and Joey had been going for the money. But how Erin and Isobel fit in—how my boss knew Isobel—I just couldn't wrap my mind around it.

"Agent Hawke?" It was one of the guys from IRD.

I wiped blood off my upper lip. Gregor's beating seemed to have resulted in a broken nose. "What's up?"

He asked me a few questions. How did I know

the witch outside the perimeter? Why had I called in Domingo Hawke instead of backup? What was Eduardo's role in what had happened here? I answered him on autopilot. Unlike the LAPD, the IRD agent actually seemed to believe me. Refreshing.

I'd witnessed the aftermath of more than a few investigations gone nasty, so the sight of the forensics team moving into The Olive Pit was actually comforting. It was so normal, in that "my life is weird" kind of way, that the residual panic from the fight finally began to subside.

The insanity of the week drained out of me, replaced the monotony of the status quo.

I stood back and watched as everything was tagged, labeled, and outlined. Ballistics experts started figuring out where all the bullets had come from. I could have told them it was pointless trying to sort that out, but nobody seemed interested in talking to me.

In fact, now that everything had calmed down, it was like I'd turned invisible. Spent a few days a fugitive and started feeling like I was important. Now Isobel and Fritz were having an intense conversation in the corner, like the kind of conversation that looked like it should happen in a locked bedroom somewhere, two IRD agents were questioning Thandy, and the photographers were taking pictures of everything but me.

I don't have much pride, but what little I had was licking its wounds.

With nothing else to do, I drifted over to Thandy. Her face crumpled when she saw me.

"I'm so sorry," she said. Blood poured out of a wound on her temple, rapidly soaking through a dishtowel pressed against it. She must have been hurt when the Union came in. The fact that it wasn't clotting made me think that she wasn't exactly human. "I only cooperated because of Erin."

"Hold up," I said. "What about Erin?"

"Gregor told me to tell everyone you were dating. He wanted them to think that you'd been beating her. He wanted you to have nowhere to hide."

Hadn't Eduardo said something about Erin, too? Something about the bounty?

"Thandy, was Erin human?" I asked.

The manager shook her head. "She was Gray, like me. We both got recruited into the Needles last year. I'm sorry. I'm so sorry."

So Thandy wasn't a full succubus—she was a half-demon, a Gray. It explained why she was bleeding so profusely. And if Erin had been a half-succubus, too, then that would explain why I had been unable to resist her sexual allure. It hadn't been chemistry. It had been thrall.

I was an OPA agent. I should have known better.

Damn.

One of the IRD agents grabbed Thandy's arm. "Do you have any other questions, Agent Hawke? We need to get her to a healing witch soon."

"No, go ahead," I said, backing away.

I watched him take Thandy upstairs with a sinking feeling in my gut. Erin hadn't gone home with me because she wanted me. She'd probably wanted to feed, and I'd been throwing myself at her feet like a giant dipshit for months.

The other IRD agent touched my sleeve. "You need to see the EMT?" he asked, squinting closely at my face through his spectacles. "You look pretty bad."

Just my shriveled pride shattering into a million pieces. Don't mind me. "I'm fine. Thanks."

I couldn't deal with the investigation anymore. I headed upstairs to the bar, snagging a bottle of wine out of the rack on my way up the stairs. I know I'd sworn to stop drinking, but it wasn't hard liquor—a little wine never hurt anybody.

Sinking into one of the leather chairs on the first floor, I uncorked the bottle and took a swig. It tasted a little peppery, kind of woody. A lot like bitter self-hatred.

Isobel took the chair next to me and reached for the bottle. "I could use some of that." Her bloody face had been cleaned and someone had given her an OPA-branded jacket that was way too big on her. She looked absolutely terrible.

I handed the wine to her. "That was pretty badass. The dead thing."

She smiled shyly around the mouth of the bottle as she sipped. "It was a new trick. It's kind of interesting how inspiring total panic can be."

Inspirational was a word for it.

"I saw security footage. You left the Glock in my apartment. Did you kill Erin?"

Isobel blushed. "No, I'd been snooping in your apartment the day before, while you were at work.

I guess I forgot it there. It was an accident."

Snooping? Just like she'd been snooping at Suzy's place?

"Who the fuck *are* you?" I asked.

"Isobel Stonecrow is a friend of mine," Fritz said, wiping the blood off of his hands with a monogrammed handkerchief as he sauntered over.

Friend, he'd said. Right. The kind of friend that you fondled after saving her life.

"We met a couple of months ago because he needed to speak to his late grandfather," Isobel said. She flashed a smile at him. "He wasn't fooled by the drums and animal skins either."

"I saw right through all of your pretense." Fritz smiled back at her. "She proved trustworthy with my grandfather's spirit. When I realized that my department had been infiltrated by the Needles, I needed someone outside the organization I could trust, and Belle was that woman. She's been investigating the Needles and all of my agents for the last several weeks."

I remembered how she'd told me that nobody called her Izzy, and now I knew why. She preferred the OPA agents wrapped around her pinkie finger to use a different diminutive.

"Ergo the snooping," she said.

Fritz was speaking to me, but he could barely take his eyes off Isobel. "I believed you were trustworthy, Cèsar, but I had to be sure. Agent Takeuchi was high on my list of suspects. You've been close with her, and you had previous connections with the Silver Needles."

"Was that why you assigned Isobel's

investigation to me?" I asked.

He nodded. "The Needles had identified Belle as my ally and a threat. I wanted to see how you handled the investigation. Unfortunately, we had that little problem with Erin Karwell first. Speaking of which…"

"Cèsar killed her in self defense, Fritz. She was a half-succubus. She attacked him," Isobel said. "Erin Karwell and her coworker, Thandy Cannon, were Gray planted at The Pit to watch the OPA." A smile flashed over her lips. "You're going to have to find another bar to hang out at after work."

Fritz looked disappointed. "I'm going to miss dollar rib night."

I was going to miss living a normal life where I thought I could trust people. But you know, priorities. "Where's Joey? Agent Dawes?"

"He'll be arrested by now. Another unit went to his house at the same time this one moved in on Costa."

Guess I should have felt relieved about that, but I was too exhausted. "So…what now? What about Agent Takeuchi? She didn't have anything to do with Erin or the Needles. Her only crime was being unlucky enough to work for the OPA."

"Ah, yes. I'll make some calls," Fritz said.

He whipped out the Blackberry and walked off again.

Isobel reached out, grabbed my hand. "I'm sorry I lied to you, Cèsar."

The memory of her kissing me in the RV flashed through my mind, shortly followed by the memory of Fritz kissing her. I got up and

WITCH HUNT

abandoned the wine bottle on the table between our chairs. "I'm gonna get some air."

"Thank you for saving me. Again."

The way she said that turned my guts to hamburger.

Not going to think about it.

I managed to tear myself away from Isobel. Walk through the swarm of OPA agents moving in and out of the building. Bump past a photographer.

Domingo was sitting outside The Pit on the tailgate of a black SUV. He was smoking again, and he hadn't smoked since getting married. When he saw me, he offered the cigarette in my direction. "Better not," I said. "I think I'm technically on the job right now."

"Your loss." He dragged deep. The end flared with light. As he blew smoke out of his nostrils, he nodded toward the window. Isobel was on the other side talking to Fritz. "That's the woman, huh?"

I sighed. "Yeah. That's the woman."

"And that's your boss, isn't it?"

"Yup."

"Tough cookies."

My thoughts involved a lot more expletives than that, but he'd gotten the gist of it. I sat on the tailgate next to him. "Your spell sucked. Everyone woke up."

"Your friends broke the circle." He patted the SUV. Its tire straddled the salt line.

I wasn't sure I'd call the Union "friends." Even if Eduardo and Joey had been double agents, I wasn't feeling real warm and tingly about that particular arm of the OPA at the moment. On the other hand, every scrap of brotherly rivalry I'd ever felt about Domingo was suddenly magically forgotten. "In case I forgot to tell you earlier—thanks for coming out to help me."

He grinned. "No problem."

Fritz and Isobel emerged from The Pit. "Ready to go?" he asked.

I stood. "Where?"

"I'm making a new task force specifically for internal investigations and special ops. You can select an agent you trust as your partner. I assumed you'd pick Agent Takeuchi. Unless there's someone else you'd like to nominate?"

"You assumed rightly, sir," I said. I glanced at my brother. "You good here?"

"I'm fine," Domingo said, taking a deep drag of his cigarette. "Go play secret agent man."

I was waiting for Suzy when she emerged from the Union detention center. It was in an underground bunker in the middle of the Mojave, probably an hour of driving from the nearest highway on narrow dirt roads. The entrance was hidden inside a big pile of black rocks. Suzy emerged looking disheveled and annoyed. Her suit was rumpled, tie loose around her neck, hair in a messy ponytail.

She stopped a few feet away from me with a dubious look.

"Hey, Suze," I said. "Bad day?"

"I've had better," she grunted.

"You've been declared innocent and the bad

guys are dead. What could be better than that?"

"Not being detained in the first place," Suzy said.

"Good point."

But she perked up a little. "So they're dead, huh?" She didn't give me a chance to explain. She didn't seem to care. "What the fuck happened with my Glock?"

"It was a mix-up," I said.

Anger flashed over her features. "Hell of a fucking mix-up."

"I'm sorry."

She shook her head. "It's not your fault." She tugged the rubber band out of her ponytail. Fine black hair fell around her cheeks. "Fuck, I need a shower."

I jerked my chin toward the pile of rocks. "What's it like down there? I've always been curious."

"You don't want to know."

Probably true. "Ready to go?"

"*Oh* yeah."

I escorted her toward the helicopter that had carried me out to the detention center. Apparently, Union regulations didn't allow aircraft to park directly on top of the underground construction, so it was a good quarter mile to the north. Fritz and Isobel climbed out as we approached and met us halfway.

"Welcome back, Agent Takeuchi," Fritz said. "You've been reassigned from the Magical Violations Department to a new task force. You're now Agent Hawke's partner and will handle special investigations."

Suzy glowered at him. "A promotion? Right when I'm getting out of a Union detention center?"

"Yes, it's a promotion. You'll have much more responsibility."

"And more pay?"

Fritz was stony-faced. "We'll see."

Which meant no.

Damn. I hadn't thought to ask for more money, but now that Suzy mentioned it, I wouldn't have minded a raise. I was going to need a new apartment—one where I hadn't killed a half-succubus—and moving wasn't cheap. I also really wanted to complete my *Star Trek: The Next Generation* collection on Blu-ray.

"I accept the promotion," Suzy said.

Fritz smiled. "Of course you do."

The helicopter's rotors hadn't slowed while we talked. It was ready to take off when we approached. Fritz moved to help Suzy into the helicopter, but she jerked out of reach, giving him the kind of look that could have started engine fires.

I stood back for a moment, letting them pick their seats, buckle in. Isobel waited with me.

A question had been nagging at me since we left The Pit, and I couldn't help but ask now that we were momentarily alone. "So you and Fritz," I said, leaning close, keeping my tone low. Nobody would be able to hear us under the helicopter.

Isobel's cheeks flushed. "Yeah, Fritz and me."

"Are you…?"

"We used to be." She quickly added, "But it's

been over for a while. I reminded him. He knows."

That probably shouldn't have made me feel as good as it did. The feeling didn't last long. Ex-girlfriend of my boss? The only woman I could date with even more guilt would be Domingo's estranged wife.

She climbed into the helicopter. I let Fritz help her up and kept my hands to myself.

I took the seat across from Isobel. "You knew I was going to be assigned to investigate you. So you knew I was coming. And you still dusted me with blister powder in the cemetery."

Isobel had the courtesy to look embarrassed again. She waited to respond until she had pulled on her headset. Her voice came in over the speakers, flat and crackling with interference. "I thought you might have been with the Needles at the time." She ducked her head and focused awfully hard on figuring out her buckles. "No hard feelings?"

Suzy was staring fixedly out the window, Fritz absorbed in his Blackberry. Both of them looked disturbed, probably for completely different reasons, but I knew they could hear us over their headsets.

I had a lot of hard feelings about this week and I didn't think I was the only one. But it was a new day, and apparently, we were coworkers now. Better to move on.

"Naw," I said. "No hard feelings."

Fritz pushed his microphone closer to his mouth. "Good, because we have a lot of work to do. I just received a report of anomalous infernal activity in Reno, Nevada, and we're the closest unit equipped for response."

"Infernal?" Isobel asked. "You mean demons?"

That wasn't the problem I had with Fritz's statement. "How the hell are we equipped? We just got Suzy out of the detention center. We haven't done any training for demons. We're barely even a team yet."

Fritz smirked. "I said internal investigation and special projects. This is special. Are you all ready?"

I was pretty sure that was a rhetorical question, but I exchanged a look with Suzy. For the first time since she'd stepped out of that bunker, there was a spark of mischief in her eye. "Born ready, sir." Of course this was the kind of thing she'd love. She rolled with the punches better than anyone else I knew.

This was going to be fun.

"Great," I said. "Let's go to Reno."

Hell of a week.

Printed in Great Britain
by Amazon